THE BEGINNING OF ALL ENDS

THE BEGINNING OF ALL ENDS

발행일 2025년 12월 25일

지은이 김세은 Agnes
펴낸이 손형국
펴낸곳 (주)북랩

출판등록 2004. 12. 1(제2012-000051호)
주소 서울특별시 금천구 가산디지털 1로 168, 우림라이온스밸리 B동 B111호, B113~115호
홈페이지 www.book.co.kr
전화번호 (02)2026-5777 팩스 (02)3159-9637

ISBN 979-11-7598-034-1 03810(종이책) 979-11-7598-035-8 05810 (전자책)

본 도서는 (주)북랩이 보유한 리코 인쇄 장비 등 자체 생산 인프라를 통해 제작되었습니다.

THE BEGINNING OF ALL ENDS

김세은 Agnes

북랩

Index

THE BEGINNING OF ALL ENDS

For my little brother-Thank you for listening to my early stories, even if you are the most annoying person I've met.

For my parents, I appreciate everything you've done for me.

Love you all so much.

Ch. 1
The World Begins to End

The world didn't end with a flash or a bang or a boom. It ended slowly, one scream at a time.

I was an ordinary person living her life in South Korea as a secretary at a little company in Seoul. I lived with my senior little brother about half an hour away from my office by subway. We lived in a little rented apartment on the edges of Seoul. And that was where I was when the world ended.

I was curled up in my bed, still dressed in my work clothes. It was nearing 11 o'clock and I was too exhausted to bother with showering right now. I could hear the faint sounds of my brother snoring in the room next to me through the paper thin walls. I was on my phone scrolling through my own web novel, An Apocalyptic Ending. It was one of the most well-known fantasy web novels for the first year of its publication. I had thousands of readers across the country waiting for my every upload. I was even making some money off it, although it wasn't enough to pay the bills, hence the day job I had. My life was near perfect, until I had a writer's block for a while. I didn't post new chapters for about 6 months, and the time and rumors meant that people quit reading, saying that they didn't want to read something that came from a sketchy person. A series that was known globally and had thousands of readers fell through the popularity ranks until there were only 11 people left reading, including me. Honestly, it didn't matter that my novel wasn't a big hit anymore. I wouldn't have cared if no one read the story. That novel was written by me, for me, because within its pages, I could live a thousand lives when I was tired of my own.

I watched the clock hit 10:59 pm and got ready to press the upload button for the newest chapter. Then there was a sudden flash of bright light from outside. Then came the screams. They were from outside. I yanked the curtains open and found utter chaos. There was a bright purple patch in the sky that emitted a white lightning. Monsters from movies and fantasy novels started to stream out of these dark patches, falling out of the sky and proceeding to destroy everything in sight. I saw enormous, scaly dragons breathing fire and various humanoid monsters howling. Screams sounded everywhere, breaking the quiet tranquility of the night. Beastly cries rang in the air.

Shut up. There is no way. Over the years, I'd rewritten and reread AAE so many times. I imagined and imagined again what my own little fantasy world would look like if it were real. I'd reread it enough times that I memorized nearly all of it. I'd agonized over every line—every description there had been a result of hours of consideration on how to depict this world inside my head. And the view in front of me? It was exactly as I had imagined. I'd described this very scene in hundreds of different ways, using dozens of adjectives. Yet none of my sentences had conveyed my vision and I thought no one would be able to see my world exactly the way I imagined it. Except everyone could see it now, just as I had wanted them to.

I decided to try something. I thought in my head 'Status Window.'A blue holograph instantly popped up in my vision and I couldn't help but let out a small yelp of surprise even though I was expecting it. There was a sharp rap at my door and I yanked it open to find Ascher, my little brother standing there. He was in a pair of trainers and a t-shirt that read: too tired to give a fuck. He opened his mouth, but I cut him off immediately.

"Do you see this?" I asked, pointing at the hologram.

"What am I supposed to see?" he asked, annoyed. "By the way, have you seen what's happening outside? I thought I was going insane. This shit's crazy. It's all over the world too." He handed me his phone. I found a picture of the same purple patch in the sky, only it was above the Eiffel Tower in Paris, France. I swiped and found a different picture that showed a patch above Tokyo Tower.

"Think 'Status Window' in your head and check it out." I told Ascher as I pulled him into my room. He gave a series of oohs and ahs before starting to make grabbing motions at the air.

Ignoring him, I finally gave a good look at my own Status Window. It Status Window read:

Name: Astoria Lee

Age: 22

Job: Author

Mana: 10/30

Health: 50/100

Strength: 10/25

Defense: 30/30

Agility: 40/40

Mental: 100/100

Fatigue: 2/20

Skills: {Mental Barrier-Lv. 1}, {3rd Eye-Lv.1}, {Sword Dance-Lv.1}, {Perfect Memory-Lv.1}

A line I'd written for AAE suddenly popped up in my mind.

{You will be able to earn skills and level them up, similar to the video games you people love. Your skills vary depending on what your talent was in your life. To survive this newly *changed world, you need to adapt to it using those skills.}*

I must have said it out loud because Ascher was looking at me like I was crazy. This was insane. The patches in the sky and the Status Window were proof that it was real. AAE was real. My head spun. I had so many feelings, but before anything else, I felt a sense of elation and excitement. In this world, I knew everything. How to survive. The events happening next. What absolutely had to be done. What must be avoided at all costs. This was, quite literally, my world. Speaking of which, why wasn't the first Quest here yet? The main plot of AAE was that everyone is assigned the same 100 Quests that they must complete in order to get the opportunity to become a god-like being.

As if on cue, there was a soft little "blip" and a new window opened itself in my vision. It read:

Quest-#1: Respond to the Environment
Difficulty: D+
Objective: Move to a safe place outside of the area you are currently in to find a place to claim as your own. Defend it from monsters until the time runs out.
Time Limit: 24 hours
Reward: 350 Astral Coins
Penalty for Failure: Death

Ch. 2

Respond to the Environment

This was crazy. AAE was real. Well, it was set in a post-apocalyptic world, so maybe that wasn't a good thing, but it's not like life before it was filled with sunshine and flowers. I was just about to explain the situation to Ascher when I heard it. A blood curdling roar. Instinctively, I wanted to bolt and hide. This was a predator beyond what I could handle now. Then the entire apartment split into two. I wasn't sure what hit it, only that something did. Ascher scrambled away from the sudden gap on the floor. The entire apartment was shaking. When the dust finally settled, I started looking for a way down. I grabbed a few face masks we had left over from the pandemic a few years back and gave one to Ascher. We put them on and clambered down from the third floor over broken bits of concrete and electric wires that sparked. I motioned for Ascher to follow me and started through the crowd. Already, the city was trashed, buildings turned to rubble and the streets full of monsters.

I could smell rubber burning somewhere. People were screaming as the monsters killed everyone around them. I dove beneath a Jeep for cover as two dragons stomped by, fighting over what seemed like a public bus full of people. The dragons, oh gods.

I had always been so annoyed that authors and movie makers either only had wing-less, leg-less Asian dragons or four-legged, winged Western ones. So I added both to my novel, imagining tribal wars between them too. I'd never actually written about the history of the two types of dragons, but I had it in the back of my mind. The dragons had stopped, scuffling right in front of me for the bus. One had blue scales and white fur, an Asian dragon. The other was a generic black and red Western dragon. This almost confirmed it. The coexistence of these two creatures was something I'd never seen except in my world. This was my world.

Shit, I've been lost in thought for too long. I looked behind me to make sure Ascher was alright. He wasn't there. In his place was the headless body of a middle aged man. I almost screamed, except I stopped myself at the last second, fearing the dragons would hear me. I couldn't very well go back and look for him with the dragons fighting in front of my nose. The other monsters were gathering around, waiting like vultures to see which dragon they could eat.

I had no choice. It's fine. He'll be okay. In order for either of us to have any chance at surviving this, there was a much urgent task to fulfill. It took some convincing and a full 10 minutes of debate, but

I finally climbed out from beneath the Jeep and began a desperate sprint away from the monsters, towards Seoul Amusement Park.

I needed to get there before I missed it. I ran from alley to alley. I dove under a car as a huge bird with a snake's tail swooshed over my head. I could hear screaming and ripping and shrieking and roaring from everywhere. But I didn't feel afraid or scared. In fact, I was excited. I could feel myself running faster than ever. A small notification popped up and I willed it to open, not wasting my breath on words. The notification read:

Fatigue levels are nearing 10, fainting or comas are possible when Fatigue level is 20.

Damn it. I need to find a place to rest and recharge. I need food, water, and a blade. G Mall was just a block to the right. I double checked to make sure my phone was zipped up in my inner pocket before running at full speed. I dashed between corpses and people begging me to help them. I jumped down the stairs 4 at a time and ran into the hunting gear department. I stopped to catch my breath. I realized that I had no idea what blade I should use for my skill {Sword Dance-Lv. 1}. Then I remembered my skill {3rd Eye-Lv. 1}. I said aloud "Activate skill {3rd Eye-Lv. 1}" The world was suddenly black then I could see every item clearly. When I focused on one weapon in particular, it told me the name, rank & abilities.

I moved down the aisles, looking for a good weapon. Then I found this.

Item: Hunting Knife (Rare)

Grade: A-

Effects: Increased strength 15, Increased agility 10, Increased fatigue 1 per minute, compatible with {Sword Dance}

I grinned as I unsheathed it and swept my hand over the edge. Perfect. A roar sounded from behind me and I realized that a Skeleton Bear had snuck up on me from behind. It was a terrifying sight to behold. The head of a bear, but the rest of its body was a bear skeleton with patches of meat and fur dangling on it.

I murmured "Sword Dance" as I stepped into an offensive stance. I could feel the buff effects of the Hunting Knife. The bear roared and charged at me. Ding! A notification opened on its own. "Left Shoulder" instinctively, I turned to the right as the bear slashed at the spot where my left shoulder was seconds ago. Ding! "Jump to the left" This must be the effect of the skill {3rd Eye-Lv. 1}. I did as it asked, then saw an opening to stab its left front leg. I took it. My body knew how to grip it and where to aim for and how to slash it to give it maximum damage.

I slashed and ran under its belly to the other side, dragging my knife across its vulnerable underbelly. I then ran under it to where the bear's heart was. Ding! "Roll to the right" I rolled and heard a crash as the bear jumped on to the spot I was just moments ago. I was getting used to fighting with my skills and my body. I ran under it again the moment it got up and drove the knife as hard as I could into where its heart was. I yanked the blade out as blood spurted out from various wounds. I ran out from between its 2 hind legs, what I didn't expect was the whip of its tail into my stomach.

I flew into a rack of throwing knives and threw them with my strength towards the bear's eyes. Unfortunately, I didn't have a skill in knife throwing and ended up nicking its nose. I decided that one more stab below the one I made on its chest would do the job. I ran full speed from the rack from its left to right, slashing a deep cut where its heart should be. The bear gave a moan and shuddered before collapsing, dead.

{3rd Eye-Lv. 1} and {Sword Dance-Lv. 1} deactivated blipped a notification. Another notification arrived: Due to excessive use the skill {Sword Dance} has been upgraded to level 2. As I was checking myself for injuries, I got yet another notification: Congratulations! You are the first being to slay a Skeleton Bear in Planet E-#1405! You have received 500 Astral Coins as a reward.

I saw another notification saying: Fatigue levels are too high, you are now falling into a deep sleep. My last thought before I lost consciousness was "Oh shit..."

I woke up from my sleep to find all my limbs attached and

functioning. I felt so refreshed and recharged. I decided to stay put here for now and check stats and see if I needed anything more from the Hunting Shop before I moved on to food, water, and shelter. "Status Window" I said and a familiar screen appeared.

Name: Astoria Lee

Age: 22

Job: Author

Mana: 10/30

Health: 90/100

Strength: 25/30

Defense: 30/30

Agility: 40/40

Mental: 100/100

Fatigue: 0/20

Skills: {Mental Barrier-Lv. 1}, {3rd Eye-Lv.1}, {Sword Dance-Lv.2}, {Perfect Memory-Lv.1}

Astral Coins: 500

Items: Hunting Knife (Rare)

I was surprised to see a new tab called Astral Coins until I remembered that I had gotten a reward for killing the bear. I clicked on the tab and it took me to another tab called Astral Shop. It was stocked full with materials, food, and weapons. In the back of my mind, I faintly registered reading about the Astral Shop in An Apocalyptic Ending. I quickly bought some food and water for 50 Astral Coins. Out of nowhere, a bottle of water and a loaf of bread dropped onto my lap. I hungrily ate all of it before standing up and surveying the damage to the shop.

Most of the items had fallen off of the racks and the bear's corpse was still here. I looked around for my Hunting Knife and found it under a shelf. I reached for it and found a hip sheath for it. I really wanted to upgrade my knife, and if my idea that this world was the world of An Apocalyptic Ending was correct, it would upgrade itself pretty soon. Blip! A notification appeared that read: Large amount of skeletal mana was absorbed. Upgrading weapon. There was a swirl of heat and light around the dagger. A second notification quickly replaced the first one, showing me my upgraded weapon.

Item: Beast Slayer (Rare)
Grade: A
Effects: Increased strength 25, Increased agility 10, Increased fatigue 1 per minute, compatible with {Sword Dance}, deals 30% more damage to Skeletal Monsters.

My eyes widened. I was glad that Infusion had worked, but this proved that Earth, Planet E-#1405, was slowly becoming like An Apocalyptic Ending. I wiped the blood and sweat off of my newly upgraded weapon as I contemplated my options. I needed to find a place to defend but to pick a place, I needed a high vantage point. Or..... I could just stay here and defend the shop. I had lots of weapons here, so if Beast Slayer broke, I could easily re-arm myself mid-battle. However, the shop was too big to successfully defend. But if I only had to hold it for a few hours.... How many hours was it that I was passed out for? How many hours were left? "Open Quest Details"

Quest-#1: Respond to the Environment
Difficulty: D+
Objective: Move to a safe place outside of the area you started in to find a place to claim as your own. Defend it from monsters until the time runs out.
Time Limit: 24 hours-8 hours remaining
Reward: 350 Astral Coins
Penalty for Failure: Death

Damn it! 8 hours was too long for me to hold off by myself with all my skill levels so low. I did some quick calculations and decided that it was around 2:00 pm the day after the start of the apocalypse. But why now? Why so suddenly? And why AAE of all the novels? A terrifying thought occurred to me then. Was I in the novel or did reality become the novel?

I shook off these thoughts "Shelter first, then ponder the meaning of life and the apocalypse" I scolded myself. I decided to make my way to the top of the G Mall. That would give me a high enough vantage point. But..... if I could go to Seoul Amusement Park, I could find a space to defend. There were plenty of small nooks and crannies there. I knew of a spot behind the Ferris Wheel.... The Ferris Wheel.

I could go into an unbroken compartment near the top and bunk there for 8 hours. I could defend that space, and when a monster came, I could break the window on the other side and jump. The swaying of the Ferris Wheel is likely to throw off the balance of any of the aerial monsters that could attack me from that height. Yes. That was the new plan.

I carefully surveyed the weapons with {3rd Eye-Lv. 1} and found a B+ Grade Shot Gun. If I infused it with mana, it could likely pierce the hide of dragons or wyverns. All I needed to do was to injure a flying monster's wing severely enough and it would leave me alone at the Ferris Wheel. I hoped. I need mana potions. They would help me increase my mana. I also need to take some new clothes. I looked at a reflection of myself on a relatively unbroken mirror shard.

My black hair was matted with blood and sweat and created a general mess around my head. My formal white shirt and dress pants were ruined with blood, sweat, and an enormous tail imprint on my abdomen from the lashing I got from the bear earlier.

I scanned the racks for some new clothes that would also raise my defense stats. I found a leather jacket and a pair of leggings that would raise my defense stats by 10 each. That was good enough for me. Now for the Shot Gun. I used Infuse on it and checked the weapon stats again.

Item: Shot Gun (Rare)

Grade: B+

Effects: Decrease mana 5 per shot, increase agility 5, accuracy rate 95%, 15% more damage towards Skeletal Monsters.

As I ran out of the shop, I bought 12 mana potions for 120 Astral Coins. I found myself grinning as I began the long run towards the amusement park. Why? Because I had reached the conclusion that, as an author, I should use what I know for my own survival. To live in this world and to enjoy this experience into my novel series.

I was going to make it through the apocalypse.

My tennis shoes slapped the pavement as I ran towards the amusement park. The sound echoed, and a lot of monsters ran around, trying to locate the source of the sound. The echo distorted the sound enough that I was able to slip past a few of them. As I poured on more speed, the sound got louder and more distinct. A chimera swiveled its head and bared its teeth at me before advancing on me.

"3rd Eye" I whispered. The chimera was an A Rank and I was nowhere near being able to handle a fight with it. "In all of the shit I could have been forced to fight with, a Chimera 3 ranks above me is not on that list." I muttered. I pivoted and ran full speed, not worrying about the sound anymore. The chimera was hot on my tail and gaining speed. I desperately ran towards the subway, hoping the chimera wouldn't be able to follow me down the narrow entrance. Boy was I wrong. The chimera burst through the entrance, making it significantly wider and infinitely more dangerous for me.

My mind whirled with a thousand different scenarios of what I could do and how it would react. Then I realized where I was. I was a block away from being under the amusement park. The grin on my face was feral as I raced away from the chimera. The monster blew a spurt of fire at me but I jumped to the side and avoided it. I ran down the track and turned a corner, the chimera hot on my tail and.....

ran into a dead end. A wall of rubble and flicking neon signs was in my face. "Oh fuck..." I muttered. I turned back and saw the chimera bare its teeth in what looked to me a terrifying grin. I knew it. I could never out-smart a chimera in its own nest. It knew I was toast and slowly advanced on me, taking its time now that I was cornered.

It let out a roar and its acidic saliva dripped onto the steps beneath it. The acid hissed and burned a hole straight into the floor. I winced and tried to think of ways to get out of this situation. Then, a light flicked out, sending the entire area into complete darkness. I heard something drop from the ceiling. The light flickered back on and I saw a guy. About my age, fit, lean, blue eyes, silver hair. That was all I registered before the newcomer said "4th Dimension."

A spot of darkness spread around him, encompassing me and him. I was too shocked to worry about who he was, because 4th Dimension was a skill that the protagonist of An Apocalyptic Ending used.

The skill 4th Dimension opens up a dimensional rift and teleports anything within its proximity into a safe space called the 4th dimension. This skill was the one of the basic 3 skills that the protagonist of AAE would use. The protagonist....

I was trying to recall all of my knowledge of the protagonist when a notification opened up in the corner of my eye. Due to an excessive period of trying to recall information, skill {Perfect Memory-Lv. 1} has been activated. Perfect Memory! Authors have to memorize details about entire worlds, so of course I would have a skill like this. I thought: Recall all information about Calix, the protagonist of AAE. Another notification blipped in response: Due to the large amount of information about: Calix, the protagonist of An Apocalyptic Ending, all information will be stored in the form of a notification.

Great! Now, if I could just take a look a-. "-lo? Can you hear me? Can you give me any sign that you are awake?" A smooth deep voice washed over me. It was cold but lyrical at the same time. I finally opened my eyes and realized that there was someone staring at me. Blue eyes. White hair that falls to his chest. But most of all? He was the exact face I had dreamed of. The character I had spent days on building.

He was the protagonist, and my masterpiece on top of that. I would spend nearly an hour closing my eyes and imagining that face. The sharp angles of his cheek bones, the scar at the corner of his eyes, the hair, the eyes, the skin, the build, and everything else. I had chosen with exact care. I had this perfect image of Calix in my head that I could never quite describe to my readers, yet here we were. Calix Nerezar, straight out of my imagination.

I was lost in thought thinking about AAE until I realized that he had asked me a question. "Oh, I'm so sorry. I must be so out of it. My name is Astoria, thank you for saving me from the chimera."

He raised an eyebrow "Chimera? How do you know what monster that is?" I searched around for a plausible excuse "I... umm... Chimera is the name of a Greek mythological monster and I thought it looked the same as in the stories." He instantly lowered his brow and replied in a smooth tone "Oh, of course. My name is Calix and I am happy to help." It was a bit odd that he was using his real name with me, but whatever. 'Open Notification-Calix, skills from chapters 2~3.' As I pretended to look around at the space the 4th Dimension created, I examined the list of skills he had.

{4th Dimension-Lv. 1}, {Eye of Truth-Lv. 2}, {World Walker-Lv. MAX}, {White Star Sword Aura-Lv. 2}

My eyes almost popped out at that last one. Wasn't he in his 2nd world? How did he already have {White Star Sword Aura-Lv. 1}? I also realized that he probably used his real name with me because he had {Eye of Truth-Lv. 2} and could get rid of me later if I lied. I took a deep calming breath. Okay, I could do this. I was literally the person who created this guy. I could handle him.

"How long can you use {4th Dimension-Lv. 1} for?" I asked him. He turned to face me completely. "How do you know this is the 4th Dimension I created?" Crap. I forgot he was extremely cautious. "I... I am a Reader as of now. When this quest ends and the second quest, the Job Change Quest arrives, I plan to be a Reader-Necromancer. I used my {Read} skill to 'read the flow of time' and I saw you." His eyes widened. I could practically see the gears turning in his head.

If I knew what the 2nd quest was, that meant I had a skill that allowed me to read the future. I had set it so that in AAE, Prophets could read all possible futures while Readers could read the flow of time and know exactly what would happen next. If this really is his 2nd world like I suspected, he needs my supposed skills as a Reader to get through the 7th quest. He knows this as well. The fact that I also know about the Necromancer is also a good sign for him. If he accepts me as a companion, I can help him, and he can help me save the world.

Blip! {Calix has activated {Eye of Truth-Lv. 2} Target selected}

There was a moment of silence as he worked his skill on me. Shit. If he found out I lied to him about being a Reader, he would most likely kill me right here, right now....

Blip! {The Target's words have been confirmed as "true" Automatically disabling the skill...}

What?! How is this possible?! I'm not a Reader. Unless...... I had a skill powerful enough to override {Eye of Truth-Lv. 2}, this shouldn't be possible. I took another deep breath and tucked that information away for later, focusing on the situation at hand.

"Sorry for not trusting you, Astoria. I just had to check. I can hold the skill for 10 minutes at my current level. We've been here for about 8. As soon as that time ends, we will end up right back where we were." Calix said coolly. "Thank you for telling me that, Calix." I said in an equally smooth voice "I know this is sudden, but would you accept me as a Companion for this world?"

Calix stared at me, stunned. And understandably so. Companions cannot lie to each other, they can sense each others' thoughts and they must protect each other for life. They can form a bond only if both sides agree but the bond can be destroyed single handedly. Or for regression, I thought bitterly. I returned my attention to Calix "I can help you in Quest 33. All I ask is that you either accept or reject before the timer for the 4th Dimension runs out."

50 seconds left on the clock

40 seconds

35...

20......

"I will accept, but grant me the right to stop the Companionship if I am not impressed by the end of the 1st Quest." He finally said.

A smirk filled my face "Deal, and trust me, you will be impressed."

Blip! {Due to the extremely prolonged usage of the skill {Perfect Memory-Lv. 1}, the skill will be forcefully updated to {Memory of the World-Lv. 2} You can now "memorize" skills that you see in your opponents and use them. Your proficiency in the skill will vary based on the level of understanding you have of your opponent.}

I added that little detail about skills updating into new skills with prolonged usage, just because I didn't like the old name for a few skills that Calix had. Thank God I did because {Memory of the World-Lv. 2} isn't a skill I directly mentioned. I had only covered it as an example when explaining the concept of it to the readers. The line popped into my head.

{For example, someone that has used one of the memory skills excessively may find that they can memorize anything, from skills to images.}

In fact, Calix does find someone with the ability to memorize and show whatever they saw because they had an Eidetic memory.

Then the 4th Dimension collapsed and spit us back out right in front of the Chimera. Somehow, the pathway to the amusement park was open again. "My end goal is to get past the Chimera to Seoul Amusement Park. If we choose one of the Ferris Wheel compartments as our safe place, we can defend ourselves against most forms of attack." I whispered to Calix.

"Got it. Follow my lead and I'll help you get there." He whispered back. I gave him a brief nod before motioning for him to take the lead.

He stood and drew his sword. His long white hair flung wildly around him. His piercing blue eyes analyzed the chimera. A white aura coated his sword as he activated his skill. The blazing fumes of the sword aura. The purest aura of them all, created from angelic and holy energy.

Blip! {You can copy the skill {White Star Sword Aura-Lv. 1} Your understanding of this skill is extremely high. Automatically updating your skill level to level 3. You can use this skill once a day for 40 minutes}

So this is the true purpose of {Memory of the World-Lv. 2} I watched as he drew the chimera's attention. Using the Companion effects, he thought to me, Stab it in the back while I hold its attention. Use whatever offensive skill you have. I sprinted behind the chimera. It turned to face me, but Calix quickly slashed at it. I could tell he missed on purpose to keep its attention on him. Focus

Astoria, I chided myself. I need to kill it to gain more titles and buffs and, most importantly, gain Calix's respect and trust.

I activated my only offensive skill and swished out Beast Slayer. It was only a rare item. Note to self, I thought, get a better weapon. I fired a shot with my gun before I leaped onto its back. I stabbed it in the back as I activated 3rd Eye.

Blip! {Head} I rolled to the side as the monster's poisonous tail stabbed the place where my head was just at. I watched as the poison melted the outer scales and fur of the chimera. Huh, so it isn't immune to its own poison. I quickly slashed at the stab wound on the chimera's back to help the poison spread faster. Blip! {Right knee} I jumped to the left as the chimera twisted its head to blast fire at me. The insane heat of the fire distorted my view so I didn't see the tail until it was right in front of me. Blip! {Heart} I just had time to think sarcastically: Wow, thanks for such an early warning, {3rd Eye-Lv.1} before I lapsed into unconsciousness.

I woke up, only to find myself lying down on a floor made of glass... way above the sky. I yelped in surprise as I tried to stand up, before a sharp pain lanced my abdomen. I hissed as I looked at an ugly scar marring my body.

"You're up" Calix said casually as if I had woken up from a nap and not recovered from getting fucking poisoned. He sat on one of the benches with empty bottles of health potion next to him. He was polishing his sword as he talked. "As you fell unconscious from the poison, you somehow managed to keep a firm hold on your blade and drag it down the chimera's side. That long wound killed it and you got all of the drops. I dragged you back the rest of the way without much trouble and now here we are."

He re-sheathed his sword and looked me dead in the eye with those piercing eyes of his "You said you were a Reader planning to be a necromancer. Not a sword master or a martial arts enthusiast. Yet while you were unconscious, you managed to kill a beast that is 2 whole ranks above you. There are 3 reasons why this could have happened." He started to tick the reasons off on his fingers. "One, you have an insanely powerful offensive weapon skill."

I cut in "I don't. I have a level 2 {Sword Dance} and my weapon is a rare rank Beast Slayer. Trust me, you can't kill a S rank chimera with that."

He raised a brow, but he must have sensed the truth in my words because he responded with "Okay, not a skill or a weapon then. Then the only plausible option....." He trailed off.

"I know what it is. I don't know who or why or how. Yet that seems like the most likely response." I said glumly.

Calix cleared his throat "Just to be clear, we are both talking about Legends, right?" I gave a nod to him.

A Legend. They were the gods in AAE. The gods and mythical beings, good and evil, of every fairytale, myth, story, and important historical event in history. They were insanely powerful, each having the power to level entire cities with just a thought. They also had the ability to issue Hidden Quests, which could make your life hell if you weren't careful. They only revealed themselves in Quest 3, where each person receives at least 1 request from a Legend to be their Successor. The more powerful a Legend, the more powerful their Successor. If you were a Successor, then, based on your rank, you could use all or some of the special skills that your Sponsor possesses. But all Legends had ulterior motives. They could easily be your savior or downfall.

I eyed Calix. People like him, who are World Walkers, are special. They are somewhere between human and Legend. Each World Walker is given the ability to start a new life in a world close to theirs every time they die. They'll be the same age as when the apocalypse arrived in their birth world. They can walk through an infinite number of worlds to try to fulfill a task to prove themselves worthy of being a Legend. Calix is the Holy Knight Successor. If he saves 100 worlds, he is allowed to become a Legend.

I finally spoke out loud "Legends will only choose Successors in Quest 9, so why would they approach me, let alone save me from death before I even have a job?" "That's what I want to know." Calix said. "I wonder who it is..." I mused. "Well, there are possibilities," Calix agreed "It might have been Go-" He was cut off as a new notification appeared in front of both of us.

Please refrain from speaking about such things before Quest 3,

or else special punishments will be added during the next Quest.

The notification disappeared as suddenly as it had arrived."I didn't know that the system was allowed to give notifications to us outside of Quests" I said after a stunned silence. Calix nodded his head grimly. "I want to check the item drop and my stats, give me a minute or two." I said to Calix as I called the status window

Name: Astoria Lee

Age: 22

Job: Author

Mana: 30/30

Health: 65/100

Strength: 30/30

Defense: 30/30

Agility: 40/40

Mental: 100/100

Fatigue: 3/20

Skills: {Mental Barrier-Lv. 1}, {3rd Eye-Lv.1}, {Sword Dance-Lv.2}, {Memory of the World-Lv.2}

Astral Coins: 1250

Items: Beast Slayer (Rare) x 1, Shot Gun (Rare) x 1, Large Mana Potion (Normal) x 12, Chimera Poison (Epic) x 10, Chimera Scales (Epic) x 20, Chimera Fangs (Epic) x 2

My eyes widened. The chimera's item drop was insane! "Let me see," Calix said as he leaned closer to me. I could smell blood and sweat all over him. His hair brushed my chest as I rattled off all the items I got. I thought about my stats now and said "Use 1 out of 12 Large Mana Potions." Blip! {Using 1 out of 12 Large Mana Potions. Your Mana has been increased to 40/40} Great! Now...

"Infuse 1 Chimera Scale per clothing item." I ordered. Blip! {Infusing 1 Chimera Scale per clothing item. Using 5 Chimera Scales. Your defense has increased to 80/80} "Hmm..." I mused aloud. If I could increase my strength stat or weapon strength.... "Oh!" I said "What now?" asked Calix in a curious tone. "Hold on, lemme try something first" I told him. "Infuse 2 Chimera Poison to Beast Slayer and 2 Chimera Poison to Shot Gun" I ordered. Blip! {Infusing 2 Chimera Poison to Beast Slayer and 2 Chimera Poison to Shot Gun. Using 4 out of 10 Chimera Poison. Beast Slayer has upgraded to Poison Dagger (Epic) and Shot Gun has upgraded to Venom Shot (Epic)}

I grinned. I couldn't help myself. It wasn't even the end of the first quest and I already had 2 Epic Class Weapons. I explained my recent development to Calix and he took it all with a stoic and logical pace. "Now," I said as I wrapped up my explanation "The million dollar question: Do you still accept me as your Companion?"

I could see him cataloging and weighing the benefits and potential harms. He finally gave a brief nod of confirmation and my spirits soared. "Now, can I ask you a favor?" I asked him. He raised a skeptical brow. "Lure in as many monsters as you can to me"

"And why would you want me to do that?" Calix asked in a curious tone. "I need to kill as many beasts as I can to increase my adaptability for the Necromancer job. If I don't it won't even be in the job options for me in the 2nd quest." I said, struggling to my feet. Calix pushed me back down with hand. I hit the ground with a thud. "Oh, fuck you" I muttered. "What was that?" Calix asked mildly. "Nothing," I snapped back. "Let me kill some monsters. I need the kills. I need to be a Necromancer!" My voice rose to a shrill pitch at the end. He stared at me dead in the eye. He must have seen something in my eyes. Desperation, maybe? Anger?

In truth, it was both. I really needed the Necromancer job. Without it, the plan I had set to survive my own world wouldn't work and I would die. Ascher would die. Calix would keep walking across the worlds. I needed this job, and to increase my chances of getting it, I need to kill something better than 1 fucking chimera! "Fine," Calix said finally. He leaned away from me and drew his sword. He opened the door to the glass cabin. "But you'd better not die here because of your foolishness. I would hate to have to step in and save you" and with that he simply left the cabin.

I watched from above as he jumped and slid his way down the Ferris Wheel. He surveyed the area for a moment before running off towards the left. Good, I was finally alone and able to use my Astral

Coins!

"Open Astral Shop," I said aloud. A new tab opened the shop. I clicked on the "Exotic Plants" section.

{Item: Firedrake-20 Astral Coins, would you like to add this item to your cart?}

{Y/N}

{Y}

{Item: Waterdrake-20 Astral Coins, would you like to add this item to your cart?}

{Y/N}

{Y}

{Item: Earthdrake-20 Astral Coins, would you like to add this item to your cart?}

{Y/N}

{Y}

{Item: Winddrake-20 Astral Coins, would you like to add this item to your cart?}

{Y/N}

{Y}

{Item: Nucleardrake-20 Astral Coins, would you like to add this item to your cart?}

{Y/N}

{Y}

I clicked on the shopping cart icon to view the items. Once I made sure I had all 5 plants, I clicked "Purchase" Blip! {You have spent 100 Astral Coins and have obtained 5 new items} I took them all out of my subspace and held all 5 seeds in my hand.

The 5 Elemental Drakes were vicious plants that attacked anything and everything around them that moved. As long as you were either completely still or too far away from it, you were fine. The Firedrake looked like an oval-shaped volcano, with glowing red streaks along the rough, dark exterior. The Waterdrake was a perfectly clear circle with tiny sparkles and streaks in it. It almost looked like a drop of sparkly water in the sunlight. The Earthdrake was rough and slightly crumbly. It didn't have a definitive shape but it was generally dark brown to black. The Winddrake was the oddest of the 5 in terms of appearance. I could feel a soft breeze swirling in my hand, but my eyes couldn't see anything in my hand. And finally, the Nucleardrake. This one was the most dangerous of them all, but looked like a normal peach pit.

I gently put all 5 of them in the pocket of my pants before drawing my dagger and opening the door. "Activate {3rd Eye-Lv. 1} and {Memory of the World-Lv. 2}" I said. I slid the door shut and inched my way down the narrow structure. "Copy skill {White Star Sword Aura-Lv. 3}" Blip! {Skill successfully copied. Will store in Memory of the World. Automatically activating skill...} A smile broke my face, it's time to get started.

There are only about 2 and a half hours left before the quest ends and the 2nd quest starts. I need to kill as many things as I can before that time ends. I finally made my way to the ground. My core hurt from the Chimera Poison, but I could tell that my health stats were already working to detoxify the poison. I twirled my dagger as I walked around the Ferris Wheel, searching for a good spot. Finally, I decided to plant them in a circle around the Ferris Wheel, placing the Nucleardrake towards the left, Waterdrake at the center, Fire drake at the right, Earthdrake and Winddrake at the back. As soon as I finished planting all 5 of them, the plants started to grow at a ridiculous speed.

In the span of about 30 seconds, they went from seed to a 10-meter-tall plant that somewhat resembled a thistle. I stood perfectly and waited for Calix to come. After about 3 minutes, he came back with what looked like all of the monsters in the Amusement Park. I watched as he pumped his muscled legs, making sure to keep just ahead of the hoard. As they approached at a rapid pace, all of the Elemental Drakes turned to the monsters.

The Nucleardrake attacked first, shooting a giant explosive at the horde. The others soon followed. I ran straight into the thick of the monsters and started to cut down as many as I could with my new skill. Blip! {Right shoulder} I dropped my shoulder and rolled back up to face another Giant Skeleton Bear. A trail of holy energy trailed my blade as I swiped at its paw. Then a huge ball of fire landed on it and I ducked out of the way, only to meet a drakon, a 9 headed dragon with 2 tails. Blip! {Jump with knees tucked} I jumped just in time for the 2 tails to swing by below me. I could see Calix at the edge of it all, not using his skills and just attacking whatever attacked him first.

At first, I was annoyed, a little help here! Then after I swung my blade for the 20th time, I could destroy a drakon in 1 slash. My clothes were stained in blood. By the time I swung my sword for the 30th time, I felt as if my arm would fall off and I cursed Calix for doing nothing. Then, as I swung my sword for the 40th time, I understood why he did nothing. I could now easily kill 2 to 3 monsters with the aura sword. I was bathed in blood and I had probably killed the most monsters out of all of the survivors so far, which made me an adequate candidate for the job of Necromancer. He was helping me achieve my goal but also staying close by so that he could protect me if worst comes to worst.

I felt touched by his sentiment. I looked around for the next monster and found.... There was none left. I quickly got rid of the 5 Elemental Drakes before turning towards the cabin to assess the damage. Then 4 drakon heads whirled past me. I sputtered, trying to find the drakon and instead found Calix leaning against the wall in pristine clothes and a pile of drakon heads next to him. I glared at him and he used his sword to flip 4 more heads my way. I slashed them all away and checked my watch. 10 minutes left until the 1st quest ends.

"You have {White Star Sword Aura-Lv.4} That is a higher level than I have." Calix noted as he sheathed his sword. I twirled my dagger around as I surveyed the area, trying my best to find a plausible excuse. "I used the items from the chimera drop to enhance my original skill." I said Calix eyed me like he didn't believe me. Still, he let the topic slide and brushed his hair behind his ear before saying "We need to be back at the Ferris Wheel in 8 minutes. The quest ends in 8 minutes." With that, he turned and marched back to the Ferris Wheel. He started to climb up the rungs. I went over to the wheel and jumped up to a little below where Calix was. I made my way up and finally pulled myself over the edge of the cabin.

"3 minutes left," I said as a way to break the silence. Calix simply nodded and continued to stare into empty space. I assumed he was looking at a window based on his focus on what appeared to be thin air for me.

2 minutes....

1 and a half minutes....

1 minute...

30 seconds....

20..

10...

9..

8..

7..

6...

5..

4...

3...

2..

1...

Blip! {Congratulations! You survived the 1st Quest! You have received 350 Astral Coins as a reward! A notification will arrive soon to congratulate you and provide you with information on the 2nd Quest}

Ch. 3
Job Change Quest

1 second passed. Then 2, 3...

A new Quest window arrived with the usual blip. I ignored it for a moment and opened my Status Window. I thought 'Invest 11 Large Mana Potions into Mana' Blip! {Investing 11 out of 11 Large Mana Potions into Mana Points. Your mana has increased to 150/150!} I smiled. All of these kills and mana points were going to pay off when I became a Necromancer. I opened up the new Quest.

Quest-#2: Job Change Quest

Difficulty: Infinity

Objective: Select a second job you think would suit you well. Based on your job selection, you will be faced with a test that lasts for 100 hours. You will have to choose a job within 10 minutes

Time Limit: 100 hours

Reward: 2nd Job

Penalty for Failure: None

I clicked next. Another notification popped up. This one read:

Please select a job from the list below:

Sorcerer

Wizard

Shapeshifter

Mage

Swords-master

Martial Artist

Communer

Healer

etc

Honestly, I was having a bad day when I wrote this chapter. The result? I wrote that there was no penalty for failure when this may quite literally be the worst Quest possible for you to fail. Not having a Legend backing you won't do much in the early Quests, but once you get past the first 40 or so, you will be obliterated by anything or anyone you fight. Legends support their Pupils more and more as the Quests go on because if you've made it this far, you could quite possibly get to the end.

I clicked etc and a much longer list came up. I scrolled through everything as fast as I could. I wonder what job he would choose. He might pick something rash like Shapeshifter.... Of course the person I am talking about isn't Calix. Rather, I am worried for my little brother. Ascher... I hadn't thought about him at all since we got separated. I instantly felt a wave of guilt. I wonder where he is... Is he even alive? I shook my head. No. He was alive somewhere. I refused to believe otherwise. “No thanks to you,” a little voice whispered in my head. I ignored it.

Finally I found the option Necromancer. My finger hovered over the selection when I noticed Calix was just sitting there. "What are you doing?" I asked him. "I'm a World Walker. I can't have a job other than that." he said matter-of-factly. I furrowed my brow. Oh, right! Calix was only on his 1st regression, and he didn't find out about the System Hack until his 65th regression. As I pondered whether or not to tell him about the System Hack, I also cataloged his behavior. He was acting almost exactly the same as he was in the novel. He would respond positively to me telling him about the System Hack. But this could potentially alter his personality and make him a different Legend.

In the end, I decided to focus on helping him and I tapped his shoulder. "What?" he snapped. "I have something to tell you. It's about a vision I had." I told him. That got his attention. "What is it?" he asked. I could tell he was eager to find out more about the future. "All World Walkers are given infinite lives and a task they must complete 100 times. Once they complete this task 100 times, they will be allowed to become a Legend. Becoming a Legend means that you are immortal and have insane powers and abilities based on what Legend you become. Your task is to save this world, Planet E-#1405, 100 times."

Calix rolled his eyes a bit. "I know all of that." He interrupted, smirking a bit.

"However, there is a catch that the World walkers don't know about." I said as if he didn't interrupt me. " If you discover and complete every single one of the 99 things I will tell you, you can become a Legend after just one regression. These 99 things are called Hacks. If you successfully complete all 99 hacks, you will obtain a System Hack that allows you to automatically complete however many worlds you had left without actually doing them. It will also reset all of the worlds that you've regressed through so far, so everything would be restored and all monsters would be gone, and everyone would come back alive with no memory of the apocalypse ever happening."

Calix's ice blue eyes widened with my every word. Then, just as quickly, they sharpened again and he asked. "How can I trust you to tell the truth?"

"Use your skill on me. I don't care." This was the truth. As long as this world was the world of AAE, the one that I'd written, these Hacks would still exist.

Blip! {Calix has activated {Eye of Truth-Lv. 3} Target selected}

I repeated my words from before. “There are 99 Hacks and by completing them all, the world walker will automatically complete the remaining worlds and the previous worlds they have walked would be reset.”

Blip! {The Target's words have been confirmed as "true" Automatically disabling the skill...}

Calix nodded slowly. I was glowing with pride, but covering it with a snide smile. Everytime I got confirmation that this world was that of AAE, I thought my heart was going to burst with pride.

"Why are there 99 Hacks and not 100?" he asked finally.

"You have to complete 1 hack per Quest, but the Legend Selection, Quest #3, doesn't have a Hack." I replied.

Calix furrowed his brow. "But it's too late to start doing these Hacks because I didn't do one for the 1st Quest."

I smiled. "You did. The 1st Hack is to take a Companion." I said.

Calix checked his watch. "We have 2 minutes left before you start the 2nd Quest. Tell me the Hack for Quest 2." he said. My smile widened. I knew my next words would blow his mind.

"World Walkers are allowed to have "Regression-Specific" jobs. Double tap on the job option World Walker and you will be taken to a new tab. Scroll down to the 2nd to last option and click it. You will then participate in the 2nd Quest and you will have completed the 2nd Hack." I said. Calix grinned. I could see him tapping at his screen. "I'm supposed to be an Angelic Warrior?" he asked. I nodded. "You have to choose Angelic Warrior to succeed the Greatest Fragment of Divinity" I responded. He nodded and tapped on the option. "Good luck," he said. "You too" I said and clicked the option {Start the Quest for Job Option: Necromancer} A flash of light and a slight pop transported me to a new world.

The new world I was transported to was something that resembled Hell. And I don't mean figuratively. It was filled with crumbling black buildings and burning fires. I hissed as a stream of lava shot up in a geyser from the reddish brown dirt. I looked around, unsure of what to do. I knew the system wouldn't help me other than allow me the use of inventory, shop, and my existing skills, so I needed to find out what to do.

I started cataloging my surroundings. Every 17 seconds, a lava stream bursts out of a random spot on the ground. Overhead, the clouds are a deep crimson and the sky is black. There are several winged forms flying around up there. There doesn't seem to be any immediate danger, but there are no visible locations to obtain resources other than the shop. And finally, the tower. It was a huge structure that very much resembled the Leaning Tower of Pisa, except that it was charcoal black, 100 stories high, and very much not leaning.

My guess was that I was in a replicated demon realm where I

would have to fight demons of varying levels and kill all living creatures on each floor before moving up a floor. There will likely be a boss-type monster at the top, maybe the demon king, that I would have to defeat to prove myself worthy of the job Necromancer. I would have to leave a literal trail of death behind me as I climbed the tower. I sighed.

First order of business, I need to check my stats. "Open Status Window" I said aloud.

Name: Astoria Lee

Age: 22

Job: Author

Mana: 40/40

Health: 100/100

Strength: 45/45

Defense: 35/35

Agility: 40/40

Mental: 100/100

Fatigue: 2/20

Skills: {Mental Barrier-Lv. 1}, {3rd Eye-Lv.1}, {Sword Dance-Lv.2}, {Memory of the World-Lv.2}

Astral Coins: 1500

Items: Poison Dagger (Epic) x 1, Venom Shot (Epic) x 1, Large Mana Potion (Normal) x 11, Chimera Poison (Epic) x 6, Chimera Scales

(Epic) x 20, Chimera Fangs (Epic) x 2

"Use 11 Large Mana Potions" I ordered

Blip! {Using 11 out of 11 Large Mana Potions (Normal) Your Mana level has increased to 150/150}

"Invest 500 Astral Coins to skill {Sword Dance-Lv.2}"

Blip! {Skill {Sword Dance-Lv.2} has increased to {Sword Dance-Lv. 7}}

"Invest 800 Astral Coins to skill {Memory of the World-Lv. 2}"

Blip! {Skill {Memory of the World-Lv. 2} has increased to {Memory of the World-Lv. 10}}

"Open shop. Purchase 20 {Fire Resistance Potions (Normal)} for 200 Astral Coins"

Blip! {Purchased 20 {Fire Resistance Potions (Normal)} for 200 Astral Coins. Storing in inventory}

"Use 1 {Fire Resistance Potion (Normal)}"

Blip! {Using 1 out of 20 {Fire Resistance Potions (Normal)} Effects will last for 20 minutes}

Great. Preparations are now complete. I started to run towards the Tower. "Activate {3rd Eye-Lv. 1} Activate {Sword Dance-Lv. 7}" I took out—A red skeleton came at me. I swung {Poison Dagger (Epic)} at it. It crumbled into dust. Blip! {Kills: 1} Blip! {You have received 10 Astral Coins} I continued to run towards the Tower. Blip! {Behind head} I turned and shot a wyvern out of the air. Blip! {Kills: 2} Blip!

{You have received 10 Astral Coins} I turned and ran again. I shot one last wyvern and came to a halt at the door of the Tower. Blip! {Kills: 14} Blip! {You have received 10 Astral Coins}

I had just made it to the entrance and I had killed 14 demon-type monsters. I smiled. This is going to be EPIC! I pushed open the door to find....

200 pairs of glowing red eyes staring at me. Time to get to work. I leaped into the middle as the doors locked behind me with a clunk. A slash of the dagger. Blip! {Kills: 20} Blip! {You have received 60 Astral Coins} A shot to a random donkey combined snake combined lady. An Empousai, I realized. Blip! {Kills: 21} Blip! {You have received 10 Astral Coins} Shrieks and howls rose above the cloud of dust and blood in the air. I jumped into the air and put my left hand on top of my dagger. "{Sword Dance-Lv. 7} 1st Form: 100 Men Decapitation Slash." I muttered.

A black crescent-moon-shaped aura blasted the heads off of 100 monsters, as promised. Sweet. With level 7, I could access up to the 7th Form. I wiped some blood off my cheek and smiled. This is the life. I'm becoming stronger and stronger. I could save Calix, Ascher, and maybe even the whole world... I laughed as I shot a poison bullet through 2 wyverns. I slashed the chest of a red skeleton. Blip! Blip! Blip! I didn't stop to check how many I had killed or how many coins I had earned. I just swung my dagger and shot my gun. It was only after that I'd become afraid of myself and the power that I had. I had become so used to killing. Did I ever feel a repulsion against killing in the first place? Was I a psychopath if I hadn't?

Finally, I shot the final demonic bat and slid to the ground. Blip! {1st floor of the Demonic Tower-Cleared! Total Kill Count: 114 Total Astral Coin Count:1,140} Blip! {Proceed to the 2nd floor?} {Y/N}

{Y}

A solid iron door without handles appeared in front of me. I pushed the doors open and stepped onto the 2nd floor.

I don't know how many days have passed. The only meaningful way to keep track of time is the floor I am on. As I finished off clearing the 64th floor, I said "Open Status Window"

Name: Astoria Lee

Age: 22

Job: Author/Necromancer (Work-In-Progress)

Mana: 520/520

Health: 320/350

Strength: 340/340

Defense: 350/350

Agility: 510/510

Mental: 160/420

Fatigue: 25/200

Skills: {Mental Barrier-Lv. 7}, {3rd Eye-Lv.10}, {Sword Dance-

Lv.13}, {Memory of the World-Lv.18}

Astral Coins: 1500

Items: Poison Dagger (Epic) x 1, Venom Shot (Epic) x 1, Large Mana Potion (Normal) x 11, Chimera Poison (Epic) x 6, Chimera Scales (Epic) x 20, Chimera Fangs (Epic) x 2

"Open Library of Memory of the World" I said again. Blip! A new tab opened up with this:

Skill Library-{Memory of the World-Lv.18}

{White Star Sword Aura-Lv.6}

{Fear-Lv.1}

{Stone Cold Heart-Lv.2}

{Aggravation-Lv.4}

{Cloning-Lv.5}

{Spear Slash-Lv.1}

{The Strength to Lift a Mountain-Lv.3}

On every 10th floor, there was a much stronger boss monster. Each time I battled a boss, I took care to copy their strongest skill but only after using {Memory of the World-Lv.18} to increase my knowledge on the monster. This let me copy as many skills that were as strong as possible.

I don't know how much time has passed. I don't know how much time is left. I don't know where this is. I don't know how it will end. I don't know where Calix is. I don't know what he is doing. I don't know if he is alive. I don't know if Ascher is alive. No, I can't afford to think about that now. It feels like I've been stuck here for years. Fighting and fighting. Killing and killing. I'm starting to lose my mind.

The only thing that helps pass the time is wondering what my skill {Mental Barrier-Lv. 7} does. I haven't tried it and I don't want to. I feel like that is the only thing keeping me sane. Wondering what that skill is. I have a sneaking suspicion that it increases my adaptability and blocks some minor mind control and thought access skills.

Honestly, there are more questions I have about this such as why does a skill exist here that I didn't create. I kept a notebook detailing all of the skills and Legends of my worldview and I never made any sort of barrier-type skill. The story is changing, and so are the people and skills inside it. It scared me to think about the possibility of a time when the Quests or Hacks might change, but there was nothing I could do about that.

Shaking off the dirty feeling of doubt, I get up from my spot on the floor and click yes to move on to the next floor. A familiar iron door greets me and I push it open to reveal yet another room full of monsters and demons. I sigh and draw Poison Dagger and Venom Shot. "Activate skills {3rd Eye-Lv.18} and {Sword Dance-Lv.13}" I leap into the air. "{Sword Dance-Lv. 13} 9th Form: Divine Emperor's Supreme Wrath." I mutter.

I swing my dagger in a now-familiar motion and an entire legion of winged demons disappear without so much as a trace of them left over. Blip! {Left Arm} I shot Venom Shot twice towards my left without looking. A quick glance tells me that it was a Chimera, but a relatively small one. Good. The monsters are stronger, but I am too. Infinitely stronger. I sighed. Just another miserable floor to clear in a miserable, seemingly endless, tower.

The hours and floors started to blur as I climbed the Demon Tower. I made my way painstakingly slowly to the top. 87th floor cleared. I thought I caught a glimpse of Ascher here. 93rd floor cleared. Nearly got impaled on a spike because I thought I heard Ascher call my name. 96th floor cleared. I wasn't capable of complete thoughts anymore. 99th floor cleared. I stared, exhausted, at the iron door that would lead to the 100th floor. I wasn't so much physically exhausted but mentally. To have no company, alone while you fought an endless stream of monsters. It made me wonder why I lived. Why do I have to go through this Hell? I stared at my new Status Window.

Name: Astoria Lee

Age: 22

Job: Author/Necromancer (Work-In-Progress)

Mana: 700/700

Health: 400/400

Strength: 630/630

Defense: 400/400

Agility: 640/640

Mental: 20/420

Fatigue: 210/370

Skills: {Mental Barrier-Lv. 7}, {3rd Eye-Lv.23}, {Sword Dance-Lv.19}, {Memory of the World-Lv.27}

Astral Coins: 2,500

Items: Poison Dagger (Epic) x 1, Venom Shot (Epic) x 1, Large Mana Potion (Normal) x 11, Chimera Poison (Epic) x 6, Chimera Scales (Epic) x 20, Chimera Fangs (Epic) x 2

There isn't any other way to keep myself entertained. I started to speak and then realized that my voice was a scratchy whisper. I cleared my throat and said hoarsely "Activate skill {Mental Barrier-Lv. 7}" Blip!{Skill activated. User's newly unlocked skill is able to help keep the user's wits about them in stressful conditions and to have a clear strategic mind. It can also block all other skills that attempt to break into the user's mind. The skill will manipulate the external skill to reveal only what the user wishes to reveal. Activate skill now? Y/N}

My eyes almost popped out of my head when I read the part about "all other skills" being blocked. I recalled that, during the 1st Quest, Calix attempted to use {Eye of Truth-Lv. 2} on me and the skill had revealed an answer that was incorrect but helped my case. That must have been this skill working. I clicked{Y} and activated the skill. Instantly I could think clearer. IF I had gotten this far, I could finish this. And once I get back, I'll look for Calix and Ascher. I need to see both of them again. I re-opened the Status Window to find that my Mental Stat was now 710/710. A skill that permanently increases such a vital stat... I needed to look into this skill. But for now, I need to take advantage of this to plan. I first restocked my supply of Aether and Fire-Resistance Potions to help me take down the boss on the 100th floor. I re-sharpened and cleaned Poison Dagger and drank a few Strength Potions just for the extra boost.

I pushed open the iron doors for the last time and found a long, dark hallway, sparsely lit by torches placed erratically along the walls. The hallway only had one door at the very end. The doors and walls were painted with the same black roses and splattered with what looked like blood. I assumed I was in the hallway that would lead me to the boss monster. Thinking back, I should have been afraid, but I wasn't. It didn't matter to me what this monster was or how much stronger it was compared to me. I need to get out of here. Without me, Calix would fail, and the world would fall. Then I realized with a jolt that I didn't particularly care whether or not the world ended, only whether or not Ascher was safe.

I made up my mind. I was going to finish this. For Ascher and Ascher only. My sweet little brother. The innocent brother that I have never failed to protect. The world and Legends would pay if a single dark hair on his head was touched. I would burn everyone if his bright eyes lost even a touch of their shining belief and hope. If even one scar broke his skin... No. I need to get out of this hellhole first.

I pulled out my weapons and walked down to the beautiful obsidian doors. The sounds of my boots hitting the floor echoed in the long hall. Clack! Clack! Clack! Clack! I exhaled and pushed the door open with a loud creaking and squeaking at its hinges. In it was...

Another room. It was decorated vise versa to the hall way outside. red painted roses on the walls with dark blood splattered all over the place. The floors were covered in a deep velvet carpet that stretched to every corner of the perfectly circular room. At the other end was a high dais with a black and red marble throne on it. The throne itself was a beauty with sharp angles and a triangular backing, large seats, and long arm rests. I expected the demon king to sit there, but the throne was empty. Instead, on the right side of the throne stood a huge demon.

The demon general... It certainly owns up to its title. Because there, beside the regal throne, was the giant horned demon general... Satan.

Now, modern concepts call Satan the "devil" They also often mistake Satan for Lucifer, the demon king. In AAE, Lucifer is the demon king, Satan is his general, and all of the rest are inferior demons who have made enough mark in history to obtain a name but no title. Lucifer is the strongest demon to ever exist, and a Pride Demon. Satan is the strongest Wrath Demon to ever exist. Demons all have different types. Pride, Wrath, Sloth, Lust, Gluttony, Greed, and Envy. If a demon doesn't have enough demonic energy and power to fit any of those 7 categories, it is then transformed to a Demonic Monster. These are monsters that I have been battling on my way up here. I haven't even faced a Lesser Demon, but I have to fight and kill Satan? That's like asking a child who just finished learning the alphabet to write Shakespeare.

I didn't have time to consider the fairness of the situation because the next thing I knew, I saw a giant flaming sword in my face. I just managed to duck and activated all of my skills. 'My name is Satan,' the demon hissed. 'You are unworthy of setting foot in my palace ever again. I must kill you, as a duty to my liege!'

"Lucky for you, I don't give a shit about your liege!" I screamed back. Satan paused mid-swing. 'How can you speak the Demonic Language?' he hissed. I dodged a blast from the fire and shot back at him "Don't know, don't care." I stepped behind him and slashed his broad back, only to find that he'd side-stepped. I grunted in frustration as Satan laughed a bone-chilling laugh. I spotted a new notification. {The effects of {Mental Barrier-Lv. 7} have blocked the mind invasive skill {Demonic Laugh-Lv. 29} used by the Demonic

General Satan} My eyes widened and my gaze collided with Satan's. 'How did you block-' I rapidly fired about 15 rounds at him as I screamed "Like I said before, don't know, don't care!" Good, I hit about 10 of the 15 rounds.

I watched the acid eat away at the dark leathery skin on his back yet even as I watched, the skin was knitting itself together even after being shot 10 times in the same area with Chimera Poison. The sheer regeneration speed of this demon is on another level. I grinned as I realized that Satan may finally provide a challenge for me to fight. I side-stepped his next slash and met his stab with my dagger. My arms shook as the sword inched closer and closer to my chest. I could see Satan's ridiculously pristine teeth practically glowing on his face. Closer... Closer...

I started to slide back towards the dais as he advanced, laughing at me. Carefully, I positioned Venom Shot right at his heart. Just as I was about to take a shot. He slammed his hilt into my gun and it spun out of my grasp. 'You think you can defeat me with such puny tactics, human?!' he roared 'I who stood by my liege's side in each and every battle he fought? I who helped my liege rise to his position today? No. I am toying with you, little human. If I wanted, I could have killed you already. I could have killed you the moment you stepped into this room.'

Shit. Holy motherfucking shit. Of course I would overestimate myself at such a crucial time?! Where's my clarity when I need it?!

Here. Clarity is here, in your mind. Think. How can you get out of this situation? He holds more strength, power, and a better weapon. Your Library of Skills is useless against him because all but one of those skills have been taken from his underlings. But that one exception is from the successor of the Holy Knight. Holy energy can triumph Demonic Energy, but are you confident your actions are of good intention? Are you confident in your other skills? Can you get to that place, where you can finish him off in one, strong, divine blow? What is this? This voice in my mind. This can't be me thinking. It feels to foreign, too forced. Almost like there is a literal voice in my mind, holding a conversation with me. I am you. To be precise, I am your skill. I am the voice of the skill {Mental Barrier-Lv.7} You can call on me even when the skill isn't activated and even when you aren't in your job as an Author. You can call me Areli.

Thump! My back hit the edge of the throne. I could see in Satan's eyes that he was enjoying himself. I screamed "Invest 30% of my Astral Coins to the Agility Stat, 20% to the Strength Stat, and 20% my Mana Stat!" Blip! {All stat points have been applied} Great. Now, I have a fighting chance. With my new found agility, ducked under the blade and found myself sliding out from between Satan's wide legs.

I scrambled towards my gun, narrowly dodging fireballs as Areli commented on my moves and gave me advice. Shift your weight to your left and crouch down as you run. Don't look down, listen and feel for the hot burst of wind. Keep your eyes glued to your target. I could feel my body instinctively obey Areli's suggestions. I could feel my senses were sharper and my movements quicker.

I finally grasped the handle of my gun again and finally spun to face Satan. My gaze scanned his body from top to bottom as Areli sorted and told me all the details I needed to know. He has more muscle mass on his right arm but equal distribution on his legs. He has a tight core which means you won't be able to trip him. However, it will be hard for him to stop or change directions quickly with those heavy horns. Those horns look coated in poison by the way. His line of vision is slightly impaired due to the fact that his horns curve down rather than up. However, even a glancing blow to your stomach could leave you half dead so be careful.

A library of information from one quick glance. How amazing? I thought. 'How dare you evade your fate, puny human?' Satan roared 'How dare you not bow before my liege's throne and accept your fate? You will die here now for impertinence against my liege!" He raised his sword over his head and swooped down. I leapt aside at the last minute and he slammed his sword deep into the carpeted floor. I swooped down and grabbed 2 relatively sharp pieces of debris and ran behind him. I stabbed both his knees from behind and jammed the sharp fragments into the wounds. His immune system worked to mend the broken bones and torn ligaments and successfully embedded the stone into his knee in the process. A small grin bloomed on my face as I watched the monstrosity of a demon waddle around and wince in pain.

What a genius way to use his ridiculously fast regeneration speed against him, Astoria. But you missed the bone of his left knee in your haste to cripple him. He is faking the injury on his left and only to surprise you later. Watch out for that.

"Then I'll make sure to cripple him on the left too!" I shouted I scooped up another couple of sharp stones and weaved between his legs. A quick slash and a moment of shoving 2 stones into 1 knee, Satan was fully crippled. 'You wench! You little human cunt! You whore, how dare to lay a hand on me?' Whore? "That gives me an idea," I muttered. I ran around the room, looking for an opportunity to shoot... Bam! Bam! Bam! A bullseye right on Satan's.... 3rd leg, shall I say? I wanted to laugh, and normally, I would've. But I was tired and getting desperate. I needed to get back to Calix as soon as possible. And Ascher too. I shouldn't have left him alone in the first place... No, regret later kill the demon now.

He seemed to recover fairly quickly though. He swung at me, screaming obscenities. My eyes widened and my pulse picked up. He was angry, and he wasn't holding back now. Duck, side-step, slash, block, jump, slash. There's no room for error, Astoria. Take him down, step by step. There is no way his regeneration speed is fast enough to regrow a limb mid-fight, right? Get rid of his sword arm and use the holy skill. I gave a non-verbal okay to Areli before jumping up to the dais.

'How dare you set foot on my liege's throne?!' Satan shrieked. "Lucky me, I don't give a fucking shit about your liege or his so-called throne" I shouted back. With that, I launched myself into the air and used gravity to my advantage as I gave a clean slice to his right shoulder. With a scream to rock the depths of hell and a clang, Satan now officially had only 1 working limb left. "Activate skill {Memory of the World-Lv. 27} Select copied skill {White Star Sword Aura-Lv. 6}!" I screamed. A flash of light, and....

Blip! {You have successfully completed the 2nd Quest-The Job Change Quest. You now have the skills of a Necromancer. Would you like to use your new skill on the Demon General Satan?}

{Y}

{Before usage, please enter a command word or phrase to collect your soul. Awaiting command word...}

Hmm.... How about "To arms"? It sounds powerful and classy at the same time. I nodded. It seemed like a solid choice. "Command phrase is selected as "To arms"" I said aloud. Blip!

{Command word selected. Once the soul is collected, user will be sent back to Earth.}

I stared at Satan's corpse and stretched my hand over it.

"To arms"

With a snap, I was brought back to Earth. 'Home, sweet, home.' I thought bitterly as I looked around at the destruction and chaos.

People hadn't finished their quest yet. Or they died trying. I brushed some debris off a large concrete slab and sat down. "Come out, Satan," I said quietly. And there he was. It was Satan, but not the one I had fought and killed. He now had 4 horns instead of 2 and he was pitch black and trailed dark smoke from his skin. He stood to his full height and opened his eyes. When I looked into them, I saw unwavering loyalty in those crystal blue orbs. "My liege," He said, kneeling before me. I ignored him for a moment and asked Areli, Can you explain my new set of skills? I could feel Areli smiling in my mind. Go to your Status Window and change your job from Author to Necromancer. You will understand then. She replied. "Open Status Window" I said aloud. My voice rang out clearly, a new melody over the cacophony of screams that seemed to echo permanently in the air. I shook off those thoughts as a familiar window opened up.

Name: Astoria Lee

Age: 22

Job: Author/Necromancer

Mana: 4865/4865

Health: 400/400

Strength: 4795/4795

Defense: 400/400

Agility: 6890/6890

Mental: 710/710

Fatigue: 0/370

Skills: {Mental Barrier-Lv. 7}, {3rd Eye-Lv.23}, {Sword Dance-Lv.19}, {Memory of the World-Lv.27}

Astral Coins: 750

Items: Poison Dagger (Epic) x 1, Venom Shot (Epic) x 1, Large Mana Potion (Normal) x 11, Chimera Poison (Epic) x 6, Chimera Scales (Epic) x 20, Chimera Fangs (Epic) x 2

I could see that the coins I paid to raise my stats had worked. It seemed that I also naturally gained and lost some points. Why did that happen? Then I recalled that AAE required payment in the form of stat points when traveling between worlds. It was a stupid system meant to weaken dimension travelers. But the fact that some of my stats improved more than I had invested meant that I was naturally growing stronger, even without the help of coins. Now for the next order of business. I clicked on the Necromancer option and the Status Window Changed.

Name: Astoria Lee

Age: 22

Job: Necromancer/Author

Mana: 4864/4865

Health: 400/400

Strength: 4795/4795

Defense: 400/400

Agility: 6890/6890

Mental: 710/710

Fatigue: 0/370

Skills: {To Arms-Lv. 1}, {Soul Library-Lv. 1}, {Soul Summon-Lv.1}, {Mental Barrier-Lv. 7}

Astral Coins: 750

Items: Poison Dagger (Epic) x 1, Venom Shot (Epic) x 1, Large Mana Potion (Normal) x 11, Chimera Poison (Epic) x 6, Chimera Scales (Epic) x 20, Chimera Fangs (Epic) x 2

As I surveyed my new Status Window, I asked Areli to explain my skills to me. The skill {To Arms- Lv.1} is taking a soul from a monster that is dead. The collected soul is called a Shadow or an Awakened and it resides in your physical shadow till you decide to take it out and manifest it. It costs 1 MP if you or your Shadows killed the creature and you are attempting the skill within an hour of its death. Any more than that and it will cost you more and more of your MP. You get a total of 3 tries to Awaken a monster. If the level gap is too big, you cannot Awaken it. The {Soul Library- Lv. 1} stores all of the souls you Awaken. The stored souls will have full loyalty to you and no one else can control them. They also can't harm each other. Over time, they'll start to think more like you and understand you better. You can use the {Soul Summon-Lv. 1} to bring souls out of your library and to Earth. Both of these skills cost you no MP. Areli replied easily.

"Satan," I said aloud. "Yes, my liege?" he asked immediately. "Bring me the largest wyvern you can find. You may kill it in order to bring it back, but you must bring it back to me within the hour." A part of me screamed at my body to move, to find Ascher, that it was already too late. But the other part, the larger part, said that having more Shadows would help look for him. I felt guilty, but sure of myself. This would help look for him faster. He's a resilient kid. He'll be okay.

Satan's eyes glowed brighter as he gave a nod and dashed up a relatively tall building, no doubt surveying the area for wyverns. I lay down on the slab and waited. I could wait for forever if it meant gaining more Shadows and growing my army.

An hour and a half later, I looked proudly at my Shadows standing in front of me. There was Satan, of course, the only one who I could converse with, I found out. Then there was a wyvern, a chimera, a 9 headed drakon, a Japanese water serpent, a mutated poisonous spider, a griffin, a 4 headed hydra, a Basilisk, a Kelpie, and a Demonic cat.

Ch. 4

Selection of Legends

Just then, I heard another voice in my head 'Astoria?' it asked "Calix?' I thought back 'Astoria, quickly, come to the east side of Han River. Now.' he said briefly 'Why? You can't have me rushing over to who knows where if you don't tell me why.' I protested. 'I have a person with me. A boy about 17. He looks just like you. Same dark eyes, ivory hair, milky skin. He says his name is Ascher and that he has an older sister named Astoria.' My heart lurched to a stop. 'Calix, ask the boy for the key to life.' I thought slowly. A moment. A heartbeat. 'He said the key to life is to believe that this too shall pass.' he reported back. My mind went blank 'That's him!' I screamed in my head. 'Keep him there, I'm on my way.' I called aloud for Paragon, my Shadow Kelpie, to give me a ride to the east side of Han River. I swung on to its back saddle-less and sucked all of the other Shadows into my shadow.

The thundering of its black hooves on the pavement was a steady rhythm. Ascher. He was alive. I need to get to him. I urged Paragon faster over the river as his hooves sprayed water all over the place. Beat, thump. Beat, thump. Finally, finally. I arrived.

I instantly spotted Calix's signature long, silvery white hair. He was emitting a subtle but powerful Holy Aura. And next to him was Ascher. His arm was bandaged and he had a wolf curled around him. "Ascher!" I shouted as I slid off Paragon. I wrapped my arms around Ascher as he melted into me. The wolf and Paragon were having an intense stare off which Paragon won and proudly snorted. "Astoria! What is that thing?" Ascher exclaimed, pointing at Paragon. "It's a long story, but I'm a necromancer and that is one of my summons." I said, not letting him go. I dismissed Paragon with a wave of my hand and he returned to my shadow. I finally stood and asked Ascher "I'm guessing by this friendly wolf that you're a Carnivore Communer?" He gave a happy nod. I turned to Calix "Thank you, for taking care of him. I trust that you were successful?"

"Clearly" he snorted. He whirled around and settled onto a rusted bench.

I summoned Satan. "My liege," he said as he kneeled.

Ascher gaped at him "It talks," he said breathlessly.

Calix stood and drew his sword. "Why is it here?" He snarled.

"My liege, shall I take care of these two? The one with the sword is emitting a hostile Holy Aura." I shot Satan a look before turning to Calix.

"I had to go up 100 floors of the Demon General's Castle and kill him to get the Necromancer title. To create a trail of death amongst the unholy. I know you had to heal 100 people in a war-stricken country. Different quests for different jobs. He's mine now, and unkillable. So don't fight each other other than sparring. Got it?" I said as quickly as possible. Calix gave a gruff nod and sheathed his sword.

Satan bowed and asked, "Then why have you called me here, my liege?"

I motioned to Calix and Ascher as I ordered him "Protect these two, no matter what." He gave a short salute and disappeared into the surrounding woods, no doubt to scout the area. I motioned for Ascher to stand and he complied. "I'm going to train you on how to best commune with a beast." I said.

I took the fox from Satan's hands and set it down. With me behind it, Ascher in front of it, Satan to one side and Calix on the other, the fox was cornered. It bared its teeth and hissed. "A cornered animal is angry and afraid. These emotions make their will to live intensify. This can be both good and bad. Use your communication skills to calm it. Then use your intense trust skill to make it trust you. Then and only then use your tame skill to make the beast bend to your will. The names of the skills might not be the same, but you get the gist of it." I lectured. Ascher nodded and stretched one hand forward towards the fox and started to talk. His eyes turned like the fox's eyes and when he spoke, it was in yips and howls. I murmured slowly to Ascher "Use its fear of us against it. Make it think you are better than us. Paint a picture. Tell it that you see us as horrible, giant monsters with unknown motives. Don't try to convince it that you are a savior or a hero. Convince it to believe that you are the safest option."

To my surprise, Calix joined in. In a soft, husky voice, he told Calix "Be calm. A rock amidst the waves. Don't show your true emotions. Be logical. Reason with the fox. Put yourself in its shoes. Use terms like "us" or "our" to signify the two of you are on the same side. Take your time, but also keep an eye on your mana levels and the fact that you need to use 2 more skills."

Ascher's eyes blinked back to normal, then his irises turned a hypnotizing shade of deep blue. Then, they blinked for a final time and the fox was calm. I motioned for Calix and Satan to step away and the fox didn't bolt. I smiled at Ascher "There's my brother. How'd it feel?"

He paused and thought before he said "It was odd. I got Lex, my wolf, after the Job Change Quest already tamed. This felt better, more wild, more satisfying. I'm still more in control of Lex than Mocha." "The fox's name is Mocha?" I asked. He nodded. I reached out to Mocha and brushed it. It stood deadly still. "Good job, Ascher." I said, just as a familiar blip sounded. I opened up the Quest window.

Quest-#3: The Selection of Legends
Objective: Choose a Legend to support you throughout the rest of the Quests. Legends are the gods of this world. Convince at least one of them to support you within the time limit. You have the opportunity to meet with as many Legends as you desire.
Time Limit: 2 hours
Reward: A supporting Legend

I clicked the next button and a new tab opened to show a list of all of the Legends. I gave a little laugh. That was it? This decision is one that will determine your chances of survival, yet all the Quest window did to explain it was to "pick a supporter"? No. This quest is so much more than that. You only get 1 opportunity to find a Supporter. Actually, the term "Supporter" is wrong here. To pick a Legend means two things: you earn their support and you can succeed their "Legend" Most people only know about the first part, hence the term "Supporter" In reality, however, the Legends are in full control. Those who prove to their Legend that they are worthy of succeeding their Legend can become a Legend of the same name. Most go from their Sponsor's Successor to a World Walker to a Legend, when the student over takes the teacher. After that, the original Legend returns to the Nether, where they cease to exist in the endless void of the world.

Anyhow, I turned to Ascher "Ascher, I advise you to take the God of All Things Wild. He can help improve your skills and range. Who you choose is up to you, but avoid anyone with the title Monarch. Got it?" He nodded and tapped something and was transported away, no doubt to talk to a Legend. "Calix, this Quest doesn't have a Hack. You know who to pick." he nodded and disappeared as well. As for me, I need the stronger Legends involved in necromancy and death. I can develop my skills as an Author well enough on my own, but I do need the help of a good Legend for my Necromancer jobs. I skimmed the list of Legends.

- God of Heavenly Lightning
- One-Eyed God of Wisdom
- One Who Has Reached Nirvana
- Origin of the New World
- First Pharaoh of the Nile
- Seller of the Brightest Light
- Sharpest Embrace in the Night
- Greatest Fragment of Divinity
- Monarch of Souls
- Monarch of Frost
- Monarch of Destruction
- Monarch of Poison
- Monarch of Dragons

- Monarch of Plagues
- King of Sin
- Torturer of the Dead
- One Who Rules the 6 Oceans
- Trickster of the 9 Worlds
- Judge of Souls
- God of All Things Wild
- Etc

As expected, the Legends didn't put their true names on the list, only their titles. Very few know a Legend's true name. Knowing a true name meant having power over that Legend, so all Legends were careful not to tell their true names to any one.

I decided that I would not talk to the Sharpest Embrace of the Night, because She could dislike Necromancers for taking what would rightfully be Her souls. Then the next best option would be the Monarch of Destruction. I clicked on the tab Monarch of Destruction and I was transported to an empty room with a desk and 2 chairs facing it. The room was a dreary gray with a steel desk and chairs. I sat in an empty chair and waited. Soon, the Monarch of Destruction teleported in. I slid out of my chair and onto the floor, putting my head to the ground in a show of defiance to His destructive power.

"I am pleased with your recognition of my power." He said in a low, deep baritone "Rise, child, and take a seat." I did as He asked and finally faced him. His skin was a deep umber color and he had dark hair in a classic army cut. He had a scar over his left cheek, across his nose and over his right eye. His eyes were a stunning scarlet. He was tall and muscular, with a dark, powerful aura around him. "So, why me?" He asked. "My lord," I began, "I am asking to be under you, to see your glorious power up close. And, if you allow it, to learn your techniques. My expertise lies with Necromancy, but I need to kill many monsters in order to grow my army. I was hoping that you could help me, my lord."

He nodded along with my explanation and asked again "But what do you wish to achieve with my help and power?" I paused, and thought for a moment. "My lord," I said slowly "Forgive if I am being impertinent, but I wish to become a World Walker and one day, a Legend. I wish to succeed a Legend." His eyes glowed brighter and I knew that he was displeased. "Little human, what is your name?" He asked. "It is Astoria, my lord." I said, unsure of why he was asking this. "Astoria, out of all of the Legends, the glorious ones and the ones where you can save the world, would you rather succeed a Legend that destroys things? Why?" He asked. I chewed on my lip as I thought about it. "My lord, I believe it is better for me to destroy with these hands rather than save. I do not want the pressure of lives resting on me and people loving and adoring me. If others love me, I could always hurt them and let them down." I said truthfully.

The Legend let out a short, harsh laugh. "You can save that for another, more pure Legend than I. Tell me your true reason." I smirked. It was just like Him to see through my empty words. 'But are they truly empty?' I quashed the rising doubt in my mind. "In all honesty my lord, only the weak seek to protect. The strong have to dominate. I believe I am more suited towards the latter." I say neutrally.

"I see you are an arrogant one, Astoria," the Monarch of Destruction said coolly. The way he emphasized my name made chills run down my back. "I'll keep an eye on you, see if you truly are one of the strong."

"Thank you my lord. Just this opportunity to have an audience with you was enough for me." I replied easily. He didn't acknowledge me, just waved his hand and the room disappeared.

I found myself back on the East Side of the Han River. I opened up the list again and scrolled through. To be honest, I knew that the Monarch of Destruction wouldn't want to give up their Legend. I just wanted to meet the gentlest Monarch to get a feel for how the other Monarchs will react. I clicked on the Monarch of the Dark Arts and found myself in the same room once again. I waited for quite some time before the Monarch finally arrived. This time, I did not lower myself. The Monarch of the Dark Arts will want to see my strength. I released a bit of mana into my surroundings to give an aura of Necromancy. Subtle, but definitely not unnoticed. I surveyed the Monarch of the Dark Arts. She was a beauty for sure, but a dangerous one. She had olive skin and long dark hair that flowed freely past her waist. She was wearing an indigo robe with a golden trim. Her eyes were milky white orbs with no pupils. Her long slender fingernails were painted black and marbled white.

I sat there and She sat across from me. Her aura expanded into a more hostile tone. I expanded mine by the same amount. She expanded hers further and made it so that enough mana was in the air around her for it to be visible to me. I used even more mana and expanded my aura as well. As my black aura and her purple aura became thick smoke in the air, I could feel her staring at me with those piercing white orbs. The mana levels got almost unbearable. My mana was most likely one of the highest in the entirety of the planet, so I knew I wasn't weak. It was just that She was ridiculously strong. The auras expanded and expanded. The mana condensed to a thick cloud and was very nearly zapping and popping with energy from the amount of hostility the 2 of us were producing. At last, I stopped and recalled my aura. I had only used about half of my energy, but there was no need for the Monarch to know that. She raised a perfect dark brow at me.

"You only used half of your mana and you are nowhere near exhausted. Why did you stop?" She asked me. I mentally smacked myself in the head. Of course the one who was regarded as the

Queen of Mana Manipulation would know about my mana levels. "I only wished to converse with you faster. After all, I only have so much time to convince you." I replied easily. "I must admit that I am pleasantly surprised that you have so much mana. That was the most mana I have encountered so far in a single mortal." She admitted.

"Thank you," I said, bowing my head slightly. "I will make this quick for both of us. I want to be able to expand my mana even more and grow my shadow army. With your expertise in mana manipulation and the Dark Arts, I hoped you would help me. I also wish to rise to the position of the Monarch of the Dark Arts, one day if you would permit me to." I held my breath. I knew that the Monarch of the Dark Arts was loyal to the Monarch of Souls to the point where She would put his needs over Hers at all times.

A coil of purple mana lashed out at me and cracked like a whip literally right in front of my eyes. I managed not to flinch as She spoke. "You dare tell me to go to the Nether before my King? You dare tell me to turn my back on Him?" She thundered at me.

"My lady, I only wish to rise to the highest position of power possible. I didn't mean any offense. It would be of the highest honor if you deemed me worthy of succeeding your Legend." I said honestly. Her white eyes quieted and when she spoke again, she was calm. "You are unworthy of succeeding me, only because you do not have the potential for the Dark Arts. Necromancy is only a miniscule part of my vast knowledge. Without knowing all of the Dark Arts, you will not be respected even if you were to become the Monarch of the Dark Arts. You will be better off seeking an audience with my King, the Monarch of Souls."

My eyes widened. "Yes, I see you know Him." nodded the Monarch of Dark Arts "Go to him and tell him that I sent you to him with my approval." I nodded but I was still dazed. "I will only overlook your impertinence once, Astoria." She said, Her eyes coming alive with fire. I managed to nod and was zapped back to Earth.

The Monarch of Souls was literally the strongest Legend and the King of the Shadow Force. Well, He was seconded, but only to the Brightest Fragment of Divinity, Calix's Sponsor and the leader of the Aether. I always thought that the two were equal in strength. However, in the novel, the Holy Knight was stronger solely because She was the Incarnation of Holiness and Good while the Monarch of Souls was the Incarnation of Evil and Vile. But if the Monarch of Dark Arts thought I was worthy, it could be worth a shot. The novel always portrayed the Monarch of Souls as the Evil Villian, but I always thought that He wasn't purely evil, just that He never shared his plans or motives. I suppose people fear what they don't know. Then I should have nothing to fear. After all, I have read this novel. With a single shaky finger, I pressed on the Monarch of Souls and was transported once again.

This was the first time I entered the room to find the Legend waiting for me instead of making me wait for them. I guess no one wanted to meet with the Monarch of Souls. I bowed low and said "My most humble greetings to the Monarch of Souls, the Leader of the Nether, the Incarnation of Evil and Vile, the Lord of the Shadow Army." He stayed silent and eyed me. I still had my head lowered, so all I saw was His dark black boots and His shadow. Oh gods.... His shadow. It was filled with monsters and creatures and nightmares and horrifying creatures beyond imagination. But the sheer number of Shadows He owned was incredible. "Take a seat. I see you're aware of my Shadows." He said. I finally looked up to see a face with short cropped black hair, black eyes with a startling ring of red fire in them, and a large sword on His back. I steeled my nerves knowing he would hate any show of weakness. I had to just shoot my shot with this one. As honest and as direct as possible. No mind games. "My King," I began "I come here with the approval and suggestion of the Monarch of Dark Arts, Queen of Mana Manipulation. I wish to become your Successor and your pupil. I aim to become a Legend of my own. WIth Calix likely to be the new Holy Knight, I am aware of your situation where you would be at a disadvantage should you remain at your position. I would be most honored to be the next Monarch of Souls should my King deem me worthy of doing so." He gave me a critical once-over. "You," He said slowly, "Worthy of being the next Monarch of Souls?" I hesitated at his slow tone. "Yes, my King " I said, uncertain of how to proceed. "You must have immense mana levels for Anesia to approve of you." He said. Anesia. That was the true name of the Monarch of Dark Arts. The fact that He revealed the true name of his second-in-command means that he's taken a liking to me. "Very well, I do see your point. Then let me pose a test of sorts. I will send out exactly 1 of my weakest Shadows. Send your best. Let them battle and see the outcome."

My eyes widened at His test. One of His weakest against Satan and a few others. Yes, this could work, but His weakest may very well be at Satan's level. I have almost no information on this guy. With a lazy flick of His fingers, a Shadow appeared in front of me. It was a Chimera. A huge one. No, huge didn't capture the entirety of the beast before me. It was almost too big for my mind to comprehend. Each of its eyes were the size of my head. And this is one of the weakest of the Monarch of Souls's army. I shook my head. I just need to prove myself against him. I summoned Satan, just him, to test how the chimera would act. Satan turned to me, but didn't completely turn his back against the chimera. The Monarch of Souls stroked the chimera's back and trailed His fingers along its flank. "This is Jeremiah, one of my favorite chimeras. He isn't my weakest soldier, but a good challenge never hurt anyone." the Monarch smiled. I looked at Satan and gave him one, crystal clear command: "Destroy it"

Satan leaped onto Jeremiah and went in swinging with his sword. A fake, followed almost instantly by a slash to the right. Jeremiah dodged was fooled by the fake but the blow glanced of its shoulder. 'Lighting fast reflexes," I thought "Satan needs to be careful" Suddenly, a voice in my head startled me "I am aware, my liege." It was Satan. Somehow telepathically communicating with me. I've never done that with the other Shadows before. It's likely due to the fact that he has a certain level of intelligence. Right away, I thought to him "Watch out of the tail, its poison will most likely kill you. I can revive you if you die, but I will run out of mana faster than the Monarch will. Watch out for the mouth as well, it breathes fire." Satan didn't respond, but I saw him taking care to avoid the tail and mouth. He slashed at the tail and managed to slice off the tip. Jeremiah let out a cry and jumped up and pinned Satan to the ground. His sword clattered out of his grip. Satan pummeled the other Shadow with his fists but Jeremiah was just too strong. I gave a wave of my hands, and summoned my basilisk. It silently snaked up behind Jeremiah and bit its left hind leg. The basilisk poison burned through the chimera and in a matter of minutes, it was all over. I was worried he wouldn't allow the use of more than one Shadow and I held my breath, waiting.

The Monarch didn't speak. He only gave a brisk nod before waving his hand. Both Satan and the Basilisk disappeared. He reached into a pocket of His black cloak. He brought out a bottle of the blackest ink I've ever seen. "This is a special enchanted tattoo ink, made personally by the Monarch of Dark Arts. Pour as much of it as you want over your skin and say the name of an animal or beast. The tattoo will transform into the beast you chose. It will move around on your skin as it pleases. For example," He pulled up the sleeve of His cloak. I let out a gasp. On his forearm was a black basilisk. Perfect, moving, and most definitely alive. "I chose a basilisk. If anyone other than me or my Successor touches Obsidian, they will die of the basilisk poison. Choose wisely. You have to use the ink within 10 minutes of exiting the Meeting Room. Once you exit, choose me, then use the tattoo ink. And one more thing. A word of caution, if I may. The voice in your head as a result of your ability as an Author. Areli, I believe? Areli will disappear completely and all the things she would have told you will become your own thoughts. Ideas and observations that you made yourself. It is a fair trade, yes?" Amazing. To receive a gift from the Monarch of Souls, no, my Sponsor was that He had accepted me as His pupil and therefore a potential Successor. I wasn't surprised that He knew I was an Author. High-ranking Legends had the ability to see people's Status Windows. Really, the only people I needed to fool were Calix and Ascher.

Without waiting for my reply, He handed me the bottle and turned away. As he made his way to a shadow, I called out "Wait!" He turned to face me once again. "Who was it that saved me from that Chimera in the tunnels?" He smiled a ghostly smile and said "Let's just say that the Devil Incarnate isn't completely evil." And with that he melted into the shadows and was gone.

I was in utter shock by the time I was back on Earth. The Devil Incarnate was what some Legends called the Monarch of Souls. He was the one who saved me. But why? Maybe he saw my potential? No, but I didn't even make any clear intentions. Then why would he have done that? I shook those thoughts out of my head and quickly selected the Monarch of Souls as my Legend. After confirming with the system, I looked at the bottle again. And I knew instantly what I wanted to choose as my tattoo. I looked down at myself, trying to figure out where to pour the ink. On my stomach, below my white crop top? No, the ink might spill on my shirt. On my ankles, below my tight pants? Right above my belt, above my weapons? I finally uncapped the bottle and poured it onto my bare right arm. I watched as the ink spread across my arm but didn't drip off. It looked like my entire arm was covered by a shadow. When the last drop of ink fell from the bottle onto my arm, I whispered to the ink "Celtic Basilisk."

I watched as the ink shifted to form a huge basilisk on my arm. It slithered around in circles over my bicep and forearms. "I'll call you Seraphis." I decided aloud. One of the reasons why I'd chosen a Celtic basilisk instead of a normal one was because Celtic Basilisks could shoot deadly poison and breath fire depending on the time of year it was. Fire during the colder months and poison during the warmer months. It was a lethal combination of deadly and beautiful. I watched in fascination as Seraphis slithered up and down my body. Wrapping herself around my torso then bicep, then settling down to become a silent, lethal anklet. I sat down and waited for a bit until... POP!

Ascher appeared in front of me. "Hey, how'd it go?" I asked him. "Give me a second lemme just confirm that I selected The God of All Things Wild and that He selected me...Okay, done" He said as he tapped at something on his screen. "Did He give you anything? A gift?" I asked. I knew what the answer was before I asked the question. If a Legend is serious about taking in a human as their successor and pupil, they will give them a gift. If the Legend has no intention of being nice to the human, they would accept the request but not give them anything. However, Pan was the God of All Things Wild. Every aspect of nature bowed to him and listened to his every command. He was one of the kindest Legends out there and I knew he'd be sincere to Ascher. I could see Ascher hesitating. His eyes were all over the place, looking everywhere except at my own eyes. He started cracking his knuckles with the thumb of each hand. A nervous habit of his since he was young. Out of nowhere, Lex appeared and started to growl at me. Blip! A notification. I opened it, and it read: The information you are asking for has been classified by the God of All Things Wild. I rolled my eyes but couldn't help the smile slowly blossoming on my lips. This message meant that Pan thought it would be useful to protect Ascher. While Pan wasn't the strongest Legend, he was still a very good friend of the Monarch of Souls and a loyal subject of the Holy Knight. The only reason he was a good friend of the Monarch of Souls was because the Monarch of Souls had saved Pan. Pan... Hmmm... I watched absent mindedly as Ascher headed off with Lex towards the remnants of the convenience store.

Every Legend had titles. It was the titles that were displayed on the list. For example, God of All Things Wild for Pan. But Pan was His true name. Knowing the true name meant you could steal all the power of that Legend and essentially become a World Walker for that Legend. You would have all of the powers but not the title and immortality. If I could get my hands on the Holy Knight or the Monarch of Souls's true names... I could have some leverage over them both. Some bargaining power. I could threaten to reveal their true name to each other. If a legend's true name was revealed to another Legend, the effect would be instant. The Legend would lose all of their power and become a shriveled version of themselves. Alive only to fulfill the sacred number of 100. All of that power would become the other Legend's. But the catch? All stats and items and skills would be transferred to their own stats, items, and skills. If the Monarch of Souls stole the Holy Knight's power, He would have his stats and items plus the Holy Knight's stats and items. But the thing with skills is that the level of the Holy Knight's ultimate skill, God's Ultimatum, would transfer to the Monarch of Souls's ultimate skill, Eclipse. The power of the strongest 2 skills combined into the Monarch of Souls's skill... The very thought of it ran shivers down my spine. As the author of AAE, I should know both of their true names. Yet I didn't. They were the only two Legends I had never truly settled on a true name for. I had a list back home on my laptop of all 100 Legends, each of their titles and true names and the myths that followed them. All the names I could think of didn't seem quite right for these two, the strongest two beings in the universe. So I never revealed it. I left it as a burning question for my readers. Never have I ever regret that decision more in my life.

A sudden pop surprised me and I shrieked as Calix appeared out of nowhere. He raised an eyebrow and I realized I had summoned half a dozen of my Shadows. I felt my face flush as I quickly dismissed them. Calix thankfully ignored both my outburst and lack of control. But the first word that left his mouth temporarily stunned me. "Who?" I couldn't very well tell him that I had become his teacher's archnemesis' first pupil in a millennia. That would cause distrust from him. Seraphis slithered up my back and radiated warmth in what I thought was a comforting manner. Seraphis. Of course. "The Monarch of Dark Arts." I said to Calix evenly. The ink was from her and my mana pool is already large. "Not the Monarch of Souls?" he asks just as evenly. I give a small snort

"Like I don't know about the tension that you're causing him right now. No, the Queen of Mana Manipulation will be a better choice. 2nd powerful, suited to my skills, and stable."

Congratulations on surviving the 3rd Quest!

You have successfully become the "Monarch of Souls's" pupil.

The information for 4th Quest will follow shortly.

This is it. The start of the Elemental Odyssey. In this world, there are 5 main elements, each of which I will have to face in the coming 5 quests. Aether first, then Air, Fire, Earth, and finally, Water. Blip! I opened the notification and found:

Quest-#4: Elemental Odyssey-Aether

Objective: You will be faced in an enclosed area with 3 people whom you are in a close proximity with. They will be your teammates. Within this enclosed area, you will have to make choices to ensure the safety and survival of you and your teammates. Make sure that you and all of your teammates survive your time together. You have 1 hour to prepare in any way you want to. The hour starts when your entire team is at the specified location for your team.

Time Limit: ???

Reward: Keeping your life for 2 days

Punishment: Death by any of the methods you may

encounter in the areas

Team: Astoria Lee, Ascher Lee, Calix Nerezar

Meeting Location: Convenience Store at Han River Area 3

Preparation Time: 1 hour

Ch. 5
Elemental Odyssey

I think I should explain to you now what the element Aether is. Aether is what fills the air around us. The excess space in the world. You can basically perceive it as the very soul and essence of the world. Now, the definition of an "element" is rather loose here. In the previous world, we had 118 elements all listed in the periodic table. Now, we have 5 elements by the definition that an element is a manifestation of raw mana that occurred due to natural causes. These 5 elements can then be harnessed by those of a certain level of mana. Aether is the strongest element of them all. It makes up everything, including the other 4 elements. If you learn how to harness Aether, you learn how to do magic. Now, here's another thing. Magic in this new world is also different from the CGI and stage magicians we used to see every day. Magic here has 2 types: light and dark. This is neither good nor evil. Just light and dark. Magic, strictly speaking, is the ability to change what exists and bend it to your will. It is to manipulate what has already been created. Magic is most often used in terms of the elements. Harnessing and using the elements is the most basic form of magic. It is the one form of magic that is neither light nor dark. It's often confused with Manifestation or even Summoning, both of which aren't even Magic. Manifestation is to create something by combining different items and elements using certain skills. Summoning is used to store and use certain things. For me, I can Summon my Shadows. However, the Art of something is something else entirely. An Art is a combination of Magic, Manifestation, Summoning, and your aura. If you learn the Art of something, you have become it. You have given every particle of your existence over to that area of powers. The Monarch of the Dark Arts got her name because she mastered every single one of the dark magics. Every aspect of it. Then she became the 2nd strongest Legend to ever exist.

Anyway, as soon as I saw the 4th Quest start, I Summoned Paragon, my kelpie, to give me a ride. Calix bent the light around us and created a Light Stallion. I arched a brow at him. He thought in my head. "My sponsor gave me some tips on how to use Aether. This is one way to do it." Just then, a creepy feeling, a sort of tingling sensation ran up the nape of my neck. My head exploded in a splitting headache as the Light Stallion and Paragon snorted and pawed at the ground. Shit. Paragon was a creature of the night and darkness. The Light Stallion was made of pure light and

Calix's holy powers. The clashing of these two creatures' energies was causing my headache. A sudden wind picked up and started whipping my hair around. I looked at the Stallion and found it crackling with energy. Paragon had wisps of mana floating off of him. I looked over at Calix with watery eyes and saw him screaming as the pain increased. If both creatures were dispelled at the same time, it might lessen the pain and the wind. If one of us were late to dispelling it, the other would be in immense pain as the opposing force crashed into their mind.

"Dispel the Stallion!" I screamed at him, hoping with all my might he would listen "3,2, 1!" I sucked Paragon back into my Shadow just as the Light Stallion disappeared. The wind and my headache died instantly. I panted and crumpled to the ground to catch my breath. I saw Calix stumble over and sit next to me. "What," he panted "the bloody hell was that! How do you have such a dark aura?" I just shook my head and mumbled something about being the Monarch of Dark Arts' prodigy. He sighed and said "Guess we'll just have to go over the old fashioned way." He reached for my hand and pulled me up. I started in the direction of the meeting location. It was a silent walk there, but luckily, Ascher was waiting there and had enough energy for the 3 of us.

"We need to practice fighting together. " I said after we caught up with each other and on all of the things that happened while we were away. Calix and I also decided, though, to let Ascher in on the

Hacks, but not the part about Regression and Legend Succession. "Agreed," Calix said, "But if you and I can't reign in our auras as we use magic, all of us are going to be seriously fucked." Ascher nodded gravely. "Can't I just use my Summons instead of dark magic?" I asked Calix. "The dark and light magics won't be as bad as the dark and light auras clashing, right?" Calix looked thoughtful, but he shook his head. "I don't know, I don't think it's ever been tried." That gave me an idea. "Give me just 5 minutes. I'll switch over to Reader and I'll check the past and the results of these sorts of experiments." Ascher noticeably brightened. "So your other job was a Reader? That's sick!" he said, bouncing around. I smiled and even Calix's mouth twitched up. Then I realized that I was lying to my own brother. The thought made me sick. What kind of sister was I? I shook my head of those thoughts as I quickly switched over to Author. I quickly went through the novel, scouring my memory for any mention at all about dark and light magics or auras clashing. I knew I'd thought of a setting where the magics would repel each other, but if I hadn't written it and the magics were clashing, that meant that the world I imagined came to life, not the one I published. Thankfully, or maybe not, I had included a short snippet about the two magics in the novel. "The magics won't interact with each other at all. Just that the auras, which are manifestations of our unique manas, clash." I reported. Ascher frowned. "That's great, but why do your eyes go like that when you're in Reader?" I furrowed my brow. "What do you mean?"

"Your eyes go completely black, like your pupil took over your eye, and then your pupil recedes but the pupil is a fiery red. Then the black takes over and your eyes are back to normal." Calix said. What the actual fuck? I've never heard about this before. Kinda creepy but cool at the same time. "Probably just a side effect from using my Reader abilities." I said, smiling. A few taps, and I was back into Necromancer. "Let's start practicing from here."

A random eagle flew at me from behind and I ducked. Calix simply sidestepped the eagle and feinted left before attempting a stab and slash motion with his aura sword. I retreated a step and then pushed forward with my dagger whirling it and then using a hunting knife Ascher gifted me to slash at Calix's chest. He met the tip of my knife with the hilt of his sword and pushed back. I gritted my teeth and tried to push back, but Calix's strength was simply too much for me. He started to grin and glanced at something behind me. I quickly summoned Larson, my Demonic Hell Cat, and Larson went to work immediately, growing from the size of a house cat to that of a tiger and engaging with Calix. That gave me enough time to turn around and find that Ascher was fighting back to back with Lex against Satan, the only one I could trust to hold back when needed. But why was Calix smiling then? I did a quick 360 and found nothing until the ground beneath my feet erupted to reveal a huge mutated centipede. What the fuck? Ascher probably controlled this from the smile that stretched across his face when he saw my predicament. No, seriously, the thing was MASSIVE. It had hundreds of legs, each covered in tiny, razor-sharp hairs and a ginormous mouth filled with rows and rows of teeth dripping with acid to put any shark's teeth to shame. They expect me to use a dagger and a knife to fight this? I felt some of my mana slipping away and I realized that Larson was having trouble keeping up with Calix. I quickly retracted Larson back into my own shadow and summoned Simile, my mutated blackwidow. Calix's face blanched when he saw Simile's pincers and 8 huge legs. The ground started to rumble again, and in reflex, I rolled to the side. The centipede leaped up and started crawling towards me, gnashing its teeth. Man, I really didn't want to use any fancy mana skills, but here I am. I quickly retracted all of my shadows and switched into Author. Ascher and Calix frowned at me, obviously confused. "Giving up so soon?" Calix called. I rolled my eyes and instead launched up into the air with my dagger into a familiar pose. "*{Sword Dance-Lv. 13} 9th* Form: *Divine Emperor's Supreme Wrath and {3rd Eye-Lv.23}*" I mutter. The world clicked into view again, and within the span of mere seconds, I registered that Calix had a few nasty scratches on his arms from fighting Larson, that Ascher had a shallow cut from Satan's sword, and that the centipede below me had a slight chink in it's exterior shell near the bas of its head. I aimed for the base as I unleashed the Supreme Emperor's Divine Wrath. Hundreds of crescent moon shapes made of my mana sliced the air, and by the time I was back down on the ground, the centipede was bleeding all over, oozing thick black blood. The centipede fell to the ground with a loud thud. Dead. I ignored both Ascher's awed look and Calix's suspicious one and marched over to the corpse. I quickly changed back into Necromancer and stopped before the corpse. I stretched a hand over the corpse and said firmly "To arms" The Shadow centipede roared and lowered its head in a sort of bow to me. And, yes, centipedes can roar in my world. I had no idea what I was thinking when I wrote that. "I'll call you..... Pete. Pete the giant mutated centipede." I said aloud. Pete gave a slight rumbling sound before I sucked him back into my shadow.

As I walked back to Ascher and Calix, I summoned Satan, who immediately fell in step with me. "Okay, I think we need to establish something before we move on from here." Calix said "Tell me, Astoria, why you can use skills that even I, a World Walker, cannot?" His voice was deadly soft as he leaned in closer to me "Why can a Reader use skills that the Holy Knight Prodigy cannot?" I didn't miss the soft emphasis on my name and my supposed job. I forced a lazy smile onto my face as I leaned back, even as my heart raced and threatened to leap out of my throat. "Let's just say that I have a skill that... Ah, allows me to copy other skills to a certain extent." Calix scoffed. "Yeah. Sure. Totally." He let the words roll slowly off his tongue, dripping with sarcasm. "Use the {Eye of Truth} if you want, I won't stop you." I said, spreading my hands. I was taking a big gamble with this. Would the skill know what I want? Could it fool Calix's skill again at this level?

To my utter shock and surprise, Calix chose not to use {Eye of Truth} on me. Maybe, it was a sign that he trusted me. He looked at me for another moment or 2 before marching back over to the convenience store, muttering about there only being a couple of minutes left. I didn't know why he was being so nice, so I half expected him to turn into a jackass later down the road. All of the sudden, I realized that I didn't tell him what the Hack was for the 4th Quest. I spoke to him in my mind, "Calix?" I could practically feel his annoyance. "What?" he snapped. All of the sudden, I just snapped.

I knew he was the protagonist but he couldn't just flip the switch like that on me. I told him "You can't do that. You can't just be nice to me and help me train, and then next minute go all psychopath on me. I don't deserve that. So either tell me what the issue is so we can work it out, or I will let you suffer through the end of hundreds of worlds to finish your journey instead of telling you the rest of the Hacks." I felt him pause for a moment, almost as if he was unsure of what to do with this new version of me.

To be honest, I have always been a little bit of a hot headed woman with a rather large touch of competitiveness. I just tried to suppress it, knowing it could get me killed one day. But now? Yeah, not playing that game any more. "I'm sorry for snapping at you and being a total 'psychopath' Now tell me the 3rd Hack." Calix said sarcastically. By then, I had marched up to him, Ascher trailing me. The nerve of this man... I smiled up at him sweetly and rose on my tip toes to get real close to him. I ignored the slight fluttering in my stomach as I watched his breath and pulse speed up. His mouth hung open just a tiny bit. I leaned even closer and breathed on to his neck "No. I won't tell you. Not with that tone of voice." I leaned back and smirked as a sort of blushing fluster took over Calix's face. Just for a moment, it felt good. Like I was standing my ground and making him listen to me, because for once, I had power. Then, the fucking psychopath came back and the moment was gone."What did you just say to me?" he asked.

"You heard me, you little fucktard." I whispered "I won't tell you what the Hack is, until you apologize. Don't try to avoid it by saying the Quest will start soon, because that's all the more reason for you to apologize faster."

"What did you just call me?"

"I called you a fucktard you little piece of self absorbed shit. Unless you're having hearing problems, I won't repeat myself again."

He stared at me like I was crazy and said "Sorry for snapping at you. I promise I won't do it again. NOT. Now could you please tell me the Hack for this quest?"

I smiled. Of course Calix wasn't going down this easy. "𐌹𐍂 𐌺𐌰𐌽 𐍃𐍀𐌴𐌰𐍂 𐌰𐌽𐌳 𐌿𐌽𐌳𐌴𐍂𐍃𐍄𐌰𐌽𐌳 𐌲𐌿𐍄𐌷𐌹𐌺 𐌾𐌿𐍃𐍄 𐍆𐌹𐌽𐌴, 𐌺𐌰𐌻𐌹𐍇." I said.

His eyes widened "How can you speak Gothic as well?" I smiled slyly "I have my ways, don't I? Now properly, again, unless you want me to make you swear it upon the River Styx and invoke The God of Heavenly Lightning's wrath." He repeated the apology again, but the glint in his eyes made me think that this would come back to bite my ass later.

"This Quest puts up in a room filled with Aether and nothing else. I simply called it a room for the lack of a better word to describe it. The Aether will expand and contract in a pattern. When it contracts, it will shrink the space so that we exist and nothing else. No air, no nothing. Then, the Aether will expand again, but this time, it will bring monsters and such for us to fight. After that, following the designated pattern, the Aether will shrink and expand over and over. Most people simply fight their way out of this. They fight a grand total of 100 monsters, taking on average 2~3 days to do so. The system gives us 3 days to get out. If we cannot, we die. If we can, no Quests for 2 days. The Hack is simple: Figure out the pattern, and simply invoke it." I said, keeping my end of the promise.

"Hmm.." Ascher says sarcastically "Definitely simple. You know, when you guys filled me in earlier, you didn't make it seem this complicated." I let out a sharp laugh. "Trust me, it gets way more complicated the longer you survive." Ascher's face suddenly fell. I felt like smacking myself in the head. Why scare an innocent kid when this is bound to already be a scary and harsh experience for him? "It's gonna be okay though, Ascher." I said, placing a hand on his forearm. "We'll push through and see this to the end, whatever that may be." He gave a nod and when his eyes met mine, I saw a spark within them. A kind of spirit, a soul, a will to live. I vowed to never let that spark go out, because that was what mattered the most. Ascher, and his little spark.

As soon as I made that oath, there was a flash of light and the Aether around us bent and shivered before expanding into a giant area. Now, it's quite an odd thing, when the Aether in the world is simply too big to accommodate the things in the world. So for a moment, all of the Aether just expands until there's nothing but Aether. Nothing but nothing. It feels like you're floating and falling and moving and still all at once. I know that we're in a giant blob of Aether, but it still feels weird.

"Woah," Ascher says before clapping his hand to his mouth "I can talk!" he exclaims. I laugh as he tests his footing in the Aether. I smile as I watch him blunder around, exploring the space. Yet when he walks past a certain point, he bounces back and falls to what looks like nothing, but the boundaries of Aether. I know I'm using all of this fancy terminology, but I only know what the book told me. And that isn't very much when actually facing the quests.

I settled in and "sat" and started to clean my blades and weapons simply because I needed something to do. Calix, who apparently decided to take his leads from me, was using his sword and training himself. Calix training is quite a sight to see. His movements are smooth and his actions precise. There is purpose in every swing of his sword. The sound of his sword singing as it slices through the air. I immerse myself in tracking his movements and skills, keeping a mental list of skills I want to try out later.

"Are you just going to stare at me or do you want to spar?" Calix smirked. He twirled his sword before sheathing it and bringing out 2 wooden swords. "I have these ready to beat your ass, little girl."

I stood up, hiding my grin with my hair. "Give me that," I said, motioning towards the practice swords. Calix tossed one over to me and I barely got into a fighting stance before he launched himself at me.

"YOU ARE DEAD, BITCH" he shouted as he began to batter me with a barrage of attacks. Blip! Right shoulder. Blip! Neck. Blip! Head. Blip! Left thigh. Blip! Chest. The notifications were endless as I blocked or dodged each stab, slash, and jab Calix threw at me. "C'mon, is that all you can do?" he taunted.

"Fine," I said as I jumped as high as I could into the air. I smiled down at Calix as I said "I needed to test out my skills before the 1st wave hit anyway."

"I forfeit!" I screamed "You fucking bastard! Stop bashing my nose!" We've been sparring for the past 10 minutes and I'm already battered and bruised. But... Calix didn't look much better. I had a broken and bleeding nose, a cut on my arm, and bruises all over my body. He had a cut on his face, a bloody nose, split knuckles, and an impressive collection of bruises. Despite that, he still smiled like a maniac.

"You lose, Astoria" he gloated. I could see Ascher cracking up not too far behind Calix.

"The Quest hasn't even started yet, but you two look terrible!" he said, rolling on the floor with laughter. I threw the practice sword at him in mock anger before taking in the situation and laughing a bit myself. I looked over to Calix and he remained stone-faced. Why? I silently tossed Calix a HP restoration potion before slowly drinking one myself. As I drank, I pondered the expression on Calix's face.

It didn't look like he was angry or annoyed at us for goofing off. In fact, he seemed like he was almost... sad. It didn't seem possible. I mean, there were moments in AAE when the death of certain characters made Calix cry but other than that, he rarely seemed sad. No. Sadness isn't it. The amount of emotion on his face is too deep for it to be something as simple as sadness. Then it hit me like a freight train. Calix was a 23-year-old. He had lost everything, his home world, his family, even the ability to properly die because he is a World Walker. To him, he was looking at the life he had lost and could never gain. A World Walker never dies. They are either stuck infinitely in a loop of trying to achieve a task 100 times, or they complete the task and become a Legend. My heart crumpled when I realized that Calix would never love again. I tossed away my potion bottle before laying down and announcing "I'm going to get some rest. You should too." I wasn't sure if I was talking to Calix or Ascher, but both of them should rest up for the 1st wave.

"What are you doing?" the Monarch of Souls rumbled "How can you fall asleep next to him, after feeling sorry for him?! Do not make me regret my decision to save your life, little Necromancer." Purple mist engulfed my vision. Shadows darting in and out of the corners of my eyes. Pure white thunder crackled in the mist. The smoke cleared and the Monarch of Souls was there again. "You do not understand, do you? That was but a fraction of my power. A power that is weakening due to him. Weaken Calix or strengthen yourself. That is the only way that I will regain my strength and maintain the balance of power between the 2 fractions. As of now, Calix is threatening to tip the balance of the council in favor of the Greatest Fragment of Divinity. So hurry, and get your job done. Speaking of which, haven't you figured it out yet? You must embrace both jobs. Don't make me regret my choices, Astoria."

I gasped as I woke up. I jumped up to my feet and did a quick

360. My heart pounded in my rib cage and my hands were shaky. I calmed myself down and took a couple of deep breaths. I was still in the Aether. Calix and Ascher were asleep. It was all just a dream.

But is it? Is there anything such as a coincidence any more, now that the Legends are involved? No. That was a direct message from my Legend, and I had to obey it. I had to grow stronger without Calix or the Greatest Fragment of Divinity noticing. Yes. That's the rational course of action for me and Ascher. Yet why was it that I couldn't tear my gaze away from Calix's sleeping form? What was in those endless, deep blue eyes of his that ensnared me so far? I shoved my feelings down. I couldn't afford to fangirl any more. Calix was a part of my reality now. He isn't a character of some novel for me to obsess over. I checked the time. We've been in the Aether for about 50 minutes now. I quickly woke up Ascher and Calix and told them "It's about to begin."

Ascher tilted his head to the side, a cute habit of his ever since we were little. "How can you tell? Is it because you're a Reader?" His eyes shone with admiration as he looked at me. I was his older sister, and I needed to protect him, but I also needed to be strict with him so that I would not make it... No. That's enough depressing shit, Astoria. I mentally scolded myself.

Aloud, I told Ascher "It's been about 50 minutes since we've been here. Don't you think something will happen once we've hit the 1 hour mark?" I gave a meaningful glance over to Calix and his eyes sparked. Ascher nodded slowly and started to pace around, exploring the boundaries of the Aether. When I looked over at Calix, he was tapping at something in the air, presumably a hologram. Moments later a black watch was fastened on his wrist.

That smart bastard. Maybe I shouldn't give such obvious hints. "Or" said a little voice in the back of my mind that sounded suspiciously like the Monarch of Souls "You could just not give him hints at all. Do what you can to keep him alive and help him at a moderate level. Ascher and your own safety comes first." I considered it. Then I considered Calix. "I won't give him any more hints from now on. Just enough so that we make it out safe and he makes it out alive." I thought to the little voice. Wait. Am I really having a conversation with my own brain? Damn. That's a new low.

"Incoming!" Ascher shouted. I almost gave myself a whip lash as I glanced in his direction. There was a wave of assorted monsters charging at us. It looked like they were all coming out of a pulsing ball of light in the distance. At the front of the pack, a mile or 2 away, was a werewolf, a dragon, a drakon, a skeleton, a zombie, and some other stuff too but that wasn't the problem. "Fuck no." Calix cursed. "How many of them are there?" The monsters were coming at us, but there wasn't an end to them; they just kept appearing and appearing and appearing. Damn it. I thought this was supposed to be an easy Quest. That's when it hit me. The notification that gave us the information on the Quest didn't have a specified difficulty level on it. I dimly heard thundering footsteps and wingbeats, accompanied by loud roars and cries. In the original novel, the difficulty level was a C. So why was there no difficulty? And perhaps more importantly, why did it deviate from the original plot.

"Astoria! Watch out!" Calix shouted. I instinctively jumped away just in time for the drakon's tail to miss me. "Where the fuck where you? You can't zone out like that you bitch!" he said. His sword slashed through a group of zombies, decapitating them all. Ascher was to my right, using his creatures and a hunting knife to fight. I watched as he managed to tame a small dragon. He would be alright on his own. Alright then. Let's get started.

A wave of my hand brings out my Summons. I only give them one order. "Kill every monster in sight." Satan salutes me with his sword and leads the rest of them off to join the fray. "*{Sword Dance-Lv. 13}* and *{3rd Eye-Lv.23}*" I think. I jump up as high as I can and use the 9th form: Supreme Emperor's Divine Wrath to take care of a drakon. A few quick slices of my dagger and a skeleton bear is gone. I don't even register the notifications that tell me to duck and dodge anymore. I've become so used to them that they have become a part of me. Melding with my thoughts until looking at my notification window during a fight becomes natural for me. Seraphis slithered up my torso and extended until her fire and venom were on the tip of my left hand. A touch from Seraphis and an entire legion of monsters goes up in flames. With her in the picture, fighting becomes almost like a game of tag, where I keep the monsters occupied with my right hand and dagger until Seraphis can tap them with my left.

But like any game, the fun always comes to an end. The monsters seem endless. We've been fighting for so long and my fatigue levels were getting dangerously high. Darn it. Darn it. We needed to move but we couldn't force a break in the wave of monsters. They were pushing us back as we tried not to let them slip behind us. "Fuck it! My fatigue and mana levels are shit!" I screamed. "My arm is starting to feel like lead over here but these fucking things won't stop!" Calix called over. Ascher chimed in "I'm almost out of mana over here!"

I grabbed a mana potion from my inventory with my free hand and tossed it over to Ascher. He took a swig of the purple liquid and stuck the rest of the bottle in a pocket for later. "Smart kid" Calix muttered under his breath as he whirled by, engaged in a fight with yet another dragon. Louder, Calix called to me "We don't have a fucking choice here any more, Astoria. I'll use my aura and end this in 5 seconds."

I tapped a cyclops on the leg with Seraphis' venom and it disintegrated. "No! You fucking idiot! If we do that, you lose your chance at this Hack!" I screamed at him. "Well then you better think of a new idea fast 'cuz I'm running on fumes over here." He screamed back. "Ascher!" I called out "Can you stay by yourself for a minute?"

Ascher yelled back "Toss me another potion and I might be able to!" Once the mana potion was safely in Ascher's pocket, I ran over to Calix, killing whatever I could along the way. "Calix," I said, my voice hoarse from all the shouting "You see that pulsing ball of light over there?" I set a couple of werewolves on fire and dashed over to Calix's side to help out with a group of wyverns. He shot me a glare which I interpreted as "I could have taken care of that on my own." I looked at him and gave him my best "I'm just trying to help" look. Aloud, Calix only said "I see it. What about it?"

"That thing lets out a wave of monsters every few minutes but that isn't its only purpose. It's a major part of the Hack in this Quest." I said to Calix.

Calix gave a brief nod before taking off in a full sprint towards the pulsing orb. I give a short taxi cab whistle and start sprinting after him. Within moments, Paragon was by my side. I swung on to the kelpie's back and rode over to Calix. I motioned for him to jump on and after a moment of hesitation, he did. With Calix situated behind me, I urged Paragon to sprint towards the orb. The monsters around became increasingly more agitated as we approached the orb.

Once we were there, we circled it a few times. "If you watch closely," Calix said as he slashed away another demon "there's some kind of pattern. Monsters release in a combination of 5 minute and 3 minute intervals." I grunted as I batted away an arrow fired from a skeleton. "Keep going," I told Calix. "Although I would appreciate it if you would get a move on with it considering that I'm trying to keep you alive as you do that."

"And you've done a wonderful job with it so far." Calix snarked back. Seraphis set an incoming arrow on fire as I took care of the skeleton that fired it. "46 times." I said to him "You own me for saving your life 46 times." Calix ignored me and turned back to studying the orb. That bitch...

"I got it!" Calix shouts. His face is filled with adrenaline and sweat. Mine was full of annoyance and blood. "Took you long enough..." I grumbled. Calix ignored me and let me steer us away as he fought the monsters off for once.

"So, what should we do next, Sherlock?" I asked as we rode back to where Ascher was dealing with the monsters. "Well," he started excitedly. "The pulsing of the ball goes in a pattern of long, short, short. Then it goes short again, before going short, long, long. It pulses long again, then goes short, short, short, and short. Then the whole thing repeats. If we decode that using Morse Code, we get a 5 letter word. D-E-A-T-H. Death." He finished triumphantly in time with a swing of his sword. "So we just "invoke" death somehow? How do you even do that?" He questioned.

"Once we get back with Ascher, I'll explain." I say, wanting to put this off for as long as possible. We sped into the fray, me setting things on fire, Calix swinging his sword. "Finally!" Ascher sighed

"You guys are back! How was the weather on Mars?" he clipped sarcastically. I laughed as we told Ascher about the code. "So then, how do we invoke Death?" Calix repeated. I bit my lip and pretended to be occupied with fighting. I felt Calix's temper rise even before he spoke. "Astoria," he said quietly, almost too quiet to hear over the sound of fighting "How do we invoke Death?"

"You die." I said simply, still not meeting their eyes. "What?" Ascher screamed "Now isn't the time for jokes Astoria! Tell us!" But how do I break it to them that we had fought for so long, so hard, yet we have to die to fulfill the Hack. "We have to die!" I screamed. "We have to die here, at the hands of these low rank monsters so that we fulfill the Hack!"

For a moment, there was silence. Well, as silent as it can get on a battlefield. "Yeah right," Calix said "Astoria, for real, what do we have to do?" I mean, it's to be expected. We fought here, holding down this spot for hours. Killing and killing and killing. For hours.

Ugh... I should have known they wouldn't trust me. Stab, duck, acid, slash... I pushed myself hard, intentionally drifting further and further away from them as I fought. I recalled all of my Summoned Shadows and shouted "Just watch me and do the same! Trust me!" I watched as a dragon swooped in close. It was descending lower and lower. It raised its head and I could see the fire building in its throat. And just as the first flames began to ignite, I jumped into its mouth.

I was on fire. Quite literally, actually. The flames scorched my body and I could smell my hair burning. Seraphis tried to protect me, covering as much of my body as she could with herself. I comforted her with my thoughts, not wanting to breathe in the smoky air. Distantly, I could hear Ascher screaming "No!" Interestingly, I think I also heard Calix scream "Fuck no! Come back here!" I laughed despite my situation. I'll tell them how stupid they sounded once all of us exit the Aether. The flames burned higher, covering every inch of my body in ashes. The smoke flooded my throat and made my eyes burn. Then the pain hit. I screamed out loud as the fire enveloped my body and burned me. Oh how it hurts! Then, I died. Unfortunately, this won't be the first Quest where I did.

I woke up with a gasp. I looked around and saw that I was back in front of the convenience store in Area 3. I ran my hands over myself. Thankfully, all of my clothes were still here and I didn't have a single burnt hair on my head. I scanned my surroundings, searching for other people. Then I gave myself a mental smack on my head. This Quest is supposed to last 2 days, but I made it out in mere hours. My health and fatigue had recovered after I died, so I stood there, looking for something to do. Then I recalled the weird Quest information. I reopened the notification:

Quest-#4: Elemental Odyssey (Partial Completion)

Objective: You will be faced in an enclosed area with 3 people whom you are in a close proximity with. They will be your teammates. Within this enclosed area, you will have to make choices to ensure the safety and survival of you and your teammates. Make sure that you and all of your teammates survive your time together. You have 1 hour to prepare in any way you want to. The hour starts when your entire team is at the specified location for your team.

Time Limit: ???

Reward: Keeping your life for 2 days

Punishment: Death by any of the methods you may encounter in the areas

Team: Astoria Lee (you), Ascher Lee, Calix Nerezar

Meeting Location: Convenience Store at Han River Area 3

Preparation Time: 1 hour

I remembered correctly. There was no difficulty level. I switched over to Author and used *{Memory of the World-Lv. 27}* "Recall all information regarding the 1st Elemental Odyssey in the form of a notification." I commanded. Blip! [The 1st Elemental Odyssey is the Odyssey of Aether. The goal was for your team of 3 to all make it out alive or the Aether Zone. The Aether Zone has a Pattern Orb, an orb which releases low-level monsters in a pulsing, continuous pattern. The hidden Hack for this Quest is based on the pattern in which the orb releases monsters. The pattern, once decoded using morse code, reveals the word DEATH. You must die in order to fulfill the Hack. After you die, you will revive in the original Meeting Location as specified by the Quest Window. There is no specific time constraint and the reward is keeping your life for 2 more days, the punishment being death by the monster waves. The difficulty level is a C.]

So I was right. The difficulty changed. But the only ones allowed to change the difficulty are the Legends. Of course it was because of a Legend. I should have known that from the moment I saw that the difficulty had changed. But which one? Who would want to test me? Or is it even about me? What if it was to test Calix? Or to kill me? Or perhaps it could be Ascher? Who might have a motive to test or kill one of us? Was it even about us three? If it was about the three of us, the Greatest Fragment of Divinity could have been the one. She knows that Calix can regress and live again. She would want to get rid of me before I help the Monarch of Souls further. But how would she know that I'm the Monarch of Souls's Successor?

But other than that, why were Calix and Ascher taking this long? Even if there was a time difference, they should have been able to die pretty quickly considering that we were overwhelmed by monsters. Does Calix not trust me? He probably wouldn't because he's the cautious type. But what about Ascher? Does he not trust me any more? Was I too strict on him over the years? Are they still fighting the monsters? Why aren't they back yet?

Pop! Calix and Ascher suddenly dropped into the space in front of me. I rose and crossed my arms as I gave them my best disapproving glare as they slowly came to. "Astoria!" Ascher shouted. He ran up and leapt into my arms. Or to be exact, he TRIED to. I sidestepped and let him crash on the ground. "Fuck! I think you broke my nose." He grumbled.

"I told you to trust me and it took you THIS long to die?" I ask. I check my watch. "It's been an hour and a half. It shouldn't have been all that hard to die with all of the monsters there!" Calix stood up and tied back his long hair as he gritted out "You can't just say that we need to die and then burn up in front of us!" He moved closer to me, staring at my eyes as if he could look directly into my soul. "You never even told us that we would be able to return." He was breathing hard by now and there was virtually no space between us.

"Does it even matter to you?" I asked quietly. "You'll re-do it all anyway, so you don't even care. I told you to trust me. I told you that these Hacks will help you. We're companions, so I'll do whatever it takes to protect you. Yet still... Still you don't fucking trust me." Both of us had our tempers soaring, the air rippled around us as our auras threatened to surface. No! That can't happen! With Ascher here, the whirlpool of our heavy auras will distort his mana! I had to shove it down, for Ascher's sake. But... I can't back down. I need Calix to treat me as his equal, not his servant. I stared right into his eyes.

Calix whispered softly into my ear "You seem to know everything about me, don't you? So tell me," he drew his sword from its sheath, shining both from the metal and the mana surrounding it. "Why do you think I don't trust you?"

What? What on earth is he talking about? "I know you don't trust me because you kept doubting me, telling me that this is a joke, ordering me to tell you what to do."

He gave a short, sarcastic laugh. "So you don't get it, do you?"

"Get what?" I gritted out between my teeth.

He snorted. "I died because I trusted you. I trusted you and I died after stabbing him" he pointed his thumb to the ground where Ascher was looking at the two of us. "I trusted you and died but you think, because you're a Reader, that you know everything. You have this set idea in your head that I do not trust anyone. You think I don't trust you, but you're ignoring the blatant truth. I'm here right now because I believed you. So you can quit your little mind games. Admit it, a small part of you was testing my trust in you when you died first, right? You can stop testing other people's trust and just worry about yourself. Open your fucking eyes Astoria. People change. Things that should have happened, reactions that you expected won't all happen for sure. So wake the fuck up and look at this world in the face!"

He breathed hard into my face. I didn't understand. No, I couldn't understand. But I knew, deep down, what he was saying. I had this version of Calix in my head, the one I knew from AAE. But he changed. The Quest changed. That's right. My goal is to change the story. To leave behind the story where everything is "saved" and create one where everything can flourish.

I spin away from the two of them, ignoring Ascher's questions and Calix's cold stare. I quickly dismiss the notification that tells me that the Quest has now completed. I need time. More than that, I need space to understand what it is I want. The original ending of the story is twisted. Calix needs to save the world over and over, regressing and regressing until he finally figures out all of the Hacks. How long does it take him? 4,781 regressions. So what happened to the 4,780 worlds he couldn't save? What happened to the last world he DID save? I can't let my world be destroyed. This is Calix's second Regression. And it'll be his last fucking one.

The first step, keep my head in the fucking game. I need to use the information I have from AAE well. However, I can't lose track of the changes that occur in reality, in the present. This is the biggest paradox of a World Walker. The more they regress, the more information they have. However, if they change the present using that information, the future changes, effectively rendering the information they had previously useless.

I can't get stuck in that paradox. I have to be smart about this. I cannot let anyone know I'm not a Reader. I should be able to keep it a secret from Ascher and Calix as long as I keep my mouth shut. Mind-invasive skills don't work on me, as far as I know.

I study Calix and Ascher far in the distance, trying to think of a way to explain my strange behavior to them. Thankfully, before I could tell them some lousy lie, a new notification appeared.

You have been granted two days that are free of Quests. You are free to do whatever you want. Your two days begin now.

This was also different. In the original novel, Calix always got at least a week between the Odyssey of Aether and the Odyssey of Air. I wasn't surprised though, because I had predicted that the Legend who had been changing the Quests would try to pull something like this. Right now though, the next Quest wasn't the problem. The real problem was the man standing a few paces away from me, glowering at me like he would gladly murder me.

For once, I was truly thankful for the companion bond that restrained him from harming me. However, I was also forbidden from harming him. Fuck the companion bond. Apparently my continued silence was a sign for Calix for him to take control. "The next 2 days," he said to me and Ascher "We'll train. We'll train like you've never trained before so that we can glide through these next 4 Quests." He turned and took a few steps away from me. All of the sudden, he paused and said "Starting now." Then, his blade was out, seemingly laughing as it cut through the air towards me.

In a flash, I had a long hunting knife in one hand and my short, curved dagger in the other. I caught the edge of his sword with my knife and pushed. He seemed surprised that his sword didn't draw blood. I used that surprise against him, immediately launching into the offense. *{3rd Eye-Lv. 23}* has activated without me knowing and gave me warnings of where to attack and when to defend. Slash, slice, block, duck, turn. I gave a quick leap back as he made a horizontal slicing motion, slicing the air between us and creating a whooshing sound. Strange. If he had used even a little of his mana in that attack, there would have been more power behind it. The ground may have erupted in shock or the wind may have blasted my face. But nothing happened. I quickly opened my senses as I danced around the edge of his reach, wanting to give myself time to process.

Then it hit me: there was no mana flow in the air. I wasn't using my mana because I knew I could crush him if I did that but why isn't he? Then he leapt up into the air , aiming to slice vertically along my body. The look in his eyes told me instantly. He wants this blood. He wants it bad enough to exploit the loop in the system regarding companions. They aren't allowed to harm each other, but what if it was an unfortunate training accident? As long as there is a system, there are loopholes, and as long as there were loopholes, they would be exploited. He wants to settle this argument using pure strength, stamina, wits, and system skills. I laughed a little at that before letting my eyes become sharp and dark. It's about time I got serious.

I charged in low, sweeping my leg out to make him fall. Low move, I know, but looking back, I think this fight was filled with desperation on both ends. I was desperate to prove myself, to myself, to Calix, to the Legends, to the whole fucking world. I think Calix wanted to reinstate himself as the stronger of the two, taking caution in the way he always does. A flick of my wrist sliced open a wound on his arm, drawing blood. "ΛN ΛccIϽЄNT," I said, as I smiled coldly at him.

He replied just as coldly. "T ҺΛΠΠЄNS" he said as he made a stabbing motion towards my chest. I whirled out of the way, feeling the ache in my muscles. He has more power and stamina than me. So this fight has to end fast.

I dashed in close and closed the gap, aiming for areas that cause maximum pain and damage. I let out my anger at Calix and my frustration with myself all into that fight. Calix matched me blow to blow, occasionally sneaking in a quick hit or two when I left a gap in my movements. I was just about to kick him in the chest when Ascher cried out "Stop it! Both of you!"

Startled by his sudden intervention, I turned mid-air to face him. Shit. His face was drained of blood and his eyes were wide with fear. "What are you doing?" he asked, pain filling his voice "The two of you are the two most precious people to me right now. You both saved my life."

I couldn't bring myself to meet his eyes. I knew why he was

reacting like this. Ascher was always the peaceful type. He never struck first and only did what was meant for his survival. That didn't mean he was weak, oh no. He killed monsters left and right without a morsel of regret. But he was only able to do that because he thought of them as "monsters." They were inhuman to him, evils to be eradicated, and so he killed them. But to see people fighting... Shit. I knew that he was going to see it happen more and more but to think I'd be the one to give him that shock...

"Shit, I'm sorry Ascher." I said to him, I wrapped my arm around him and rested my head on his. He was stiff for a moment before giving in to my warm embrace. I felt the sorrow radiating off of Calix. He never had a true family, so he probably felt jealous of our sibling bond. To my utter shock and surprise, Ascher waved Calix over before pulling him in close to me as well. I froze, startled at the sudden contact from him. His skin was surprisingly warm as his chiseled arms circled both me and Ascher. Soft locks of long, silver fell from his back onto my face. "We promise we won't fight, okay?" Calix murmured. Ascher was quiet for a moment, but he quietly nodded.

We stayed like that for some time. Me sandwiched between the two most important people of my world. I couldn't help but admire the irony in being embraced by the reality I hated for being my reality and the story I hated for being just that. A story.

I pulled out from between them and flipped a switch. I needed to get a grip on the situation. Ascher's eyes also hardened and wisps of his signature deep green mana encircled his hand. Calix caught on too, albeit a bit later than us siblings. His blue tinged white mana gathered at his fingertips. My own purple tinged black mana whirled around my wrist as Seraphis encircled my forearm, ready to strike as needed. Our auras feeded off of each other, growing stronger and brighter. I realized that this was Ascher's goal-to prove he could keep up with us in terms of mana but he simply chose to not be violent. He probably wanted to prove that he was stronger than we thought.

It was a good sign that he was trying to prove himself, but there needed to be some sort of realization in him that he was still weaker than me and Calix and that we could protect him. I sent my thoughts over to Calix, being careful not to allow any other thoughts or emotions to slip through our companion bond. He sent back his response, a cold "Okay" in a way that was just as careful as mine. I had a feeling that this awkwardness between us would continue beyond today. Simultaneously, we pushed our mana to the max, pressing upon the aether in the air with it. The plants in the area all withered and died then flourished as Calix's mana replenished what mine stole. Ascher's mana also rose in time with ours, albeit a bit slower but soon, he also kept up with us, expanding his mana, calling animals to the scene. Mana works like that. Everyone's mana has a different color and effect on the world. Most people have mana that just barely reacts with the world. As your mana grows stronger, the effect it has becomes stronger. Of course, depending on the individual's level of skill and control in handling their mana, the effect changes. Right now, me and Calix were both making sure that our mana wasn't reacting in any other way than growing in size and intensity of color.

Eventually, Ascher's mana began to slow its growth, swirling but not expanding or becoming more vibrant. On the other hand, Calix's ice white aura and my black-purple aura grew faster and faster, climbing and swirling and interacting with each other, throwing sparks in the air. Ascher killed his mana flow and watched us as we kept at it. Finally, Calix's flow began to slow. So this was his limit. I still had about 10% of my mana left, so I knew that I had more mana than him at least. Unless he was faking running out of mana. That would be a whole other set of trust issues. "Issues that you don't have time for," I reminded myself. I cut my mana as well, having seen my point made.

Ascher, apparently, understood what I meant because he said "Yeah. Point made. You two are crazy strong. Got it. But you have got to treat me as a human being. I'm not a helpless child. I can carry my own weight in a fight. You saw that right?"

I couldn't help but hold in a laugh at his child-like behavior. The rants that he went on still seemed so cute to me. Both Calix and I nodded at him before Calix took control of the situation again.

“Okay,” he said facing us, “We need to get a solid fighting style going between us. The best strategy would be to have me at the center and have Ascher on my right and Astoria on my left. I fight mainly with my right arm so I can easily reach over to help Ascher if needed and Astoria can hold her own. This way, even if we fight against multiple enemies, Astoria’s Shadows and Ascher’s bonded animals can help on both sides.”

It was a solid strategy and it didn’t take long before we settled on that fighting style, with me and my shotgun-dagger combo, Calix with his sword, and Ascher with his hunting knife. We decided it would be best to practice hand-to-hand combat without Shadows or animals to make things fairer for Calix. Most Summoners or Communards don’t learn combat and rely on people like Stone Skinners or Tanks to shield them. In our case, we only had 3 people so everyone needed to excel in everything. We decided to have Satan fight Ascher and for me and Calix to duel. Tomorrow, we would start fighting together, against nearby creatures or the Shadows.

I squared off with Calix once again. Surprisingly, he made the first move, leaping through the air and flying at me with his sword. I could feel that he was swinging at full strength, mana and a touch of... was that killing intent? A smile bloomed on my face. Game on, Calix.

And like that, two whole days passed and we learned to fight together, albeit a bit roughly. There were still some occasions when my dagger or Ascher's hunting knife collided with Calix's sword, but overall, we were getting used to each other's movements. Early the morning of Quest 5, we grouped together and shared breakfast from the staples stolen from the convenience store. We had a steady rhythm going between us at this point, light banter all around. There was still an undercurrent of hurt and mistrust between me and Calix but it wasn't as bad.

Just as we finished our meal, a new Quest window appeared out of nowhere.

Quest-#5: Elemental Odyssey-Air
Difficulty: Infinity
Objective: Survive assaults from the various forms of the element Air with your team.
Time Limit: 24 hours
Reward: {Blessing of Air-Lv. 3}, 250 Astral Coins
Punishment: Death
Team: Astoria Lee (you), Ascher Lee, Calix Nerezar

I made sure to check with *{Memory of the World-Lv. 27}* to check with the original book that the Quest details were correct. This one, however, had an infinite difficulty level even in the novel. The difficulty ranged from a walk in the park to being dragged through the fiery gates of hell depending on where you were.

Aside from all of that though, I had to take a moment to appreciate the reward. This Quest's reward was always amazing. It's one of the few Quests where the reward is sweeter than the risk. The skill that they gave out as a reward is one that made it much easier to use your mana to control air. The fact that they give it to you just for surviving a day is amazing. But the fact that it's already up to level 3 makes it way more useful. The hidden catch to this sweet, sweet reward is the fact that the reward changes to coins after the first 100 people get the skill. The amount of coins you get decreases as time goes by and will decrease further if your team gets injured.

I told all of this to both Calix and Ascher, and added "The Hack for this Quest is to clear the Quest in less than 10 hours."

Ascher, frowning, asked "How the hell are we supposed to do that if the Quest says to survive for a whole day?"

Calix was silent for a moment before asking, "Are we supposed to stop time? Perhaps acquire a skill that does that? Or gain help from a Legend related to time?"

I laughed at the thought of asking the lofty Light Legend Era or the moody Dark Legend Timera for help in clearing the Quest. I couldn't help the smirk on my face as I told Calix "There's no way the Time Keeper or Guardian of the Endless River would help us. The Time Keeper exists due to the people who set their clocks wrong and the Guardian of the Endless River exists because of the people who always know the correct time. Neither of them would be able to help, not to mention they both couldn't care less."

"Then what would you have us do, Ms Genius?" Calix snipped.

"That's easy," I said slowly, as if stating the most obvious thing in the world "Just survive by eliminating the threat. That's a surefire way to 'survive' the assaults."

Ascher burst out laughing "So," he said barely managing to wipe away his tears "To stop being hunted, hunt the hunter?" He laughed again. I couldn't help but smile at his child-like reaction. I could tell that he was exaggerating his joy to mask any friction between me and Calix.

Suddenly, the sound of Ascher's laughter got cut off, almost like someone hit the mute button on him. His mouth was open and moving, but no words could be heard. An air vacuum had formed around us. I saw Ascher hand stopped talking and was sticking his arm out, as if he was trying to feel the air. I glanced over to Calix and saw that he was setting a 10 hour timer using Ascher's phone. I called my mana to my fingers and motioned for Calix and Ascher to do the same. I casted a thin, protective layer of mana over Ascher before creating the same shield over myself and Calix. Ascher frowned a bit but cast a layer over me before covering himself and Calix as well. Calix casted a protective barrier around all of us simultaneously, settling the silent dispute between us siblings.

Soon, sparks began to fly into the air as Calix's mana started to fight off the air magic around us. Wind began to pick up, blowing my and Calix's hair around. The wind grew into a massive tornado, whipping trees out of their roots. I started to feel Calix's mana break and when I looked over, Calix was sweating and gasping for breath. I instantly knew what was happening. The wind wasn't just any wind-it was a Curse Cyclone.

Each Legend can decide what kind of curse to imbue to the Curse Cyclone after the item is bought. Apparently whoever had been watching our team decided that a Mana Eater would be a good curse. A Mana Eater is a curse that will become the death of anyone without an aura. All skills need mana to be used and a Mana Eater destroys mana. However, an aura can protect mana from a Mana Eater. In our case though, Calix and I can't use our auras at all, or we'll only add to the wind. Ascher on the other hand has an unstable aura, which means using it is dangerous for all of us.

I waved my arms to get Ascher and Calix's attention. I motioned as best as I could "Undo the mana shield!" I thought to Calix through our bond "Undo the mana, there's a Mana Eater loose here. Stop giving it mana to feed on and it'll destroy itself." Ascher thankfully understood my wild hand signals and immediately took his mana back. Calix, already looking pale from the mana loss, also did the same. I also withdrew my mana and grabbed a mana potion for Calix to drink. The wind was picking up and the Mana Eater, without any mana to eat, was turning on itself and destroying the mana of the Curse Cyclone.

In a flash, the wind died down and I was able to hear again. I heard Calix through our bond "I won't question how you knew that was a Mana Eater imbued Curse Cyclone. But I am curious how you knew how to destroy a Curse Cyclone. Even I didn't know about it until my second Regression."

Verbally, he only said "Thanks." One word, spoken gently to me but not meant for my ears. It was meant to grace Ascher's ears and let him know that we were working on our relationship. But through our bond, words as sharp as a dagger meant to pierce me and draw the line between us. I knew that it was partially my fault that he was acting like this, but I couldn't help but become hurt at his words.

I swallowed my words and just responded "Later," to him through our bond I just smiled at him. Then I turned to Ascher, but he was nowhere to be found. "The second phase has started." I told Calix. I made sure to feel the winds for any more Mana Eaters before I sent a wave of mana rippling out. One small burst of mana spread from me, the black circle of mana growing, allowing me to sense Calix's mana right in front of me. It also let me sense his mana disappear.

One moment, I could feel the cold of his mana and see a wisp of ice blue. Next thing I knew, it was gone. Even if you don't use your mana, it should be felt by other mana. So where was he? The second phase was the wind whisking away your group members. Once you got within visible range of each other, the wind would shove you back away from each other. If you managed to get together with your whole team, the wind would bring poison clouds to us, creating a vacuum seal until you broke the seal or died of the poison. If you didn't die, you'd have to face an Air Sprite and survive. All within 24 hours. Or in our case, 10 hours.

I spread out my mana further and felt a tickle of sunshine. I could feel that it was Ascher without looking. I began to run towards the feel of his mana. As I ran, the wind picked up, hurling shards of broken glass and entire trees my way. I flicked my wrist, pulling up shields of mana to block the flying objects. I could feel my mana levels slipping, but I needed shield and sense Ascher at the same time. Finally, through the dust and wind, I could see a figure, wandering the area with a green mana shield. "Ascher!" I yelled over the wind. By some miracle, he heard me and turned. "We need to capture the wind! Wind wants to be free! To defeat it, it needs to be trapped!" I screamed. He nodded, although I'm not sure he completely understood. With my mana, I scribbled in the air 'Cover me from there, okay?' He quickly figured out how to use his mana to write and drew a giant green smiley face. I laughed a little at his antics before I drew all my mana back to me. My shield dropped and my senses dulled once again. The wind seemed to sense my weakness, blowing faster and throwing sharp objects this way and that. Thankfully, Ascher summoned his wolf, Lex, and his fox, Mocha, to protect me. They bounded up into the air, using their teeth and claws to snatch nails and arrowheads out of the way while Ascher set up layers of mana shields around the three of us.

Great. Ascher was doing his part of protecting me, so I needed to do my part and contain the wind. I drew out about half of my mana, and molded it to create a translucent cube of mana. Now for the hardest part. There wasn't a lot said about the 5 Elemental Odysseys in AAE, only general comments about the elements. **{The elements all have a consciousness. They live and breathe and attack and defend and have feelings, just like any plant, animal, or beast.}** All I need to do is hurt their consciousness. I used more of my mana to expand my cube so that it encompassed most of the wind. It seemed to understand what I was doing and moved out of the box. I quickly changed my cube into a huge half sphere and slammed it down over the wind.

I pressed my mana down hard against the ground before shrinking the sphere. The wind beat against my mana struggling to be set free from its cage. Most of the wind around us died down and Ascher ran over to me. He grabbed a half full mana potion from his pocket and handed it to me. I downed the potion in one go and focused on shrinking the sphere bit by bit. Ascher stayed by my side, watching me with eyes filled with awe. I ignored him for the moment and kept at it, making sure the wind was confined to a smaller and smaller area. The wind beat against my mana, becoming more and more frantic as I shrunk the space. Wind loves to be free. It wants freedom and open space. So how do you stop it from being a threat to you? You take away its freedom and confine it.

I smiled as the wind kept fighting me. With the mana potion Ascher gave me, l was upping the pace a bit, not afraid of mana loss. The wind was becoming a tornado at this point, but looking at it, it seemed desperate rather than angry.

Then suddenly it just stopped. The wind died, literally. I made sure it was completely gone by crumpling my mana sphere like a sheet of paper. It was quiet around us again. Ascher asked "How the hell did you do that?" His eyes were bright, staring at me with such awe. I smiled and explained to him what I had done. "So," he said slowly after hearing my explanation "You just made the wind commit suicide."

I frowned at that but I couldn't correct him because he was right. Just as I opened my mouth, a familiar voice cut in "Astoria did what?" I turned and found Calix walking over to us. Shit. If he reached us, he would trigger the start of the third phase.

"Calix!" I shouted "Stop! Whatever you do, don't fucking move!"

Immediately, he froze. "Why?" he called back.

"If you come close to us, you trigger the start of the third phase!"

"There are phases to this fucking thing?" Ascher groaned.

"What is the third phase? How many phases are there? Can we do anything to prepare for the phases?"

"The wind will bring a poison cloud to our whole group before sealing it, and us, into a sphere of wind. There's four phases total, we just finished the second one over here."

"The second phase was making forcing the wind to commit suicide?" Calix asked, laughing a bit.

"No, we just need to eliminate the threat and that was the best way I could think of. I'll tell you later just don't move from there."

"Okay, so what do I need to do?"

"You both know how to open up the shop right?" Nods all around. "Open up the shop and buy yourself a pair of {Sea Monkey Lungs}"

"A pair of what?"

"{Sea Monkey Lungs} they help you breathe underwater and can filter out poison." I opened up my shop and bought a pair for myself using 15 coins.

{You have spent 15 Astral Coins on {Sea Monkey Lungs}. Remaining Astral Coins: 735.}

The item looked strange in my hands, like a miniature pair of slimy green blue lungs with a tube attached to the center. Ascher and Calix both made a face at the color and feel of it. I placed the item in my mouth, gently biting the end of the tube to keep it in place. Ascher made a loud groaning sound but eventually placed his own pair into his mouth. It took Calix the longest to get over placing a pair of lungs in his mouth, but he ultimately did. I motioned for

Calix to approach us, telling him in my mind "Sprint over to us and go into a defensive stance to protect Ascher as soon as you come within reach of us." He gave me a look that said "Of course," before doing just that.

As soon as he came near me and Ascher, the wind picked up again, swirling around us, enclosing us into a sphere. We were getting whipped around up in the air and the sphere of wind rose 10 meters into the sky. I think I heard Ascher screaming and I prayed with all my might that he had kept the lungs in his mouth as he did. Suddenly, there was a particularly warm gust of air that whooshed into the sphere. The wind died down instantly, only strong enough to maintain the spherical form and hold our weight. I motioned to breathe in through your mouth and out through your nose. The warm air probably carried poison. I seemed to be right because the air got warmer and warmer as time went on. The sound of our breathing seemed loud within the sphere. A wheezy intake through the sea monkey lungs, a sigh out the nose. We stayed like that for who knows how long, each of us lost in thought. On my skin, Seraphis was sending me waves of joy, probably her delight at being around so much poison. As the air passed the point of warm into hot, I covered myself with a thin layer of mana in case the poison could affect my skin. Seraphis wasn't too happy about that and curled up into a double chain on my bicep. Ascher noticed my new mana armor first and quickly did the same, Calix following suit a moment later. Finally the wind sphere holding us disappeared and the air returned into a normal temperature again. Then we fell.

It was a 10 meter drop from our cozy poisonous sphere in the sky to the surface of Earth. During that instant before we dropped, Calix covered himself in his aura while Ascher and I called on our Summons to catch us. I swung onto my wyvern's back with ease, watching from the sky as Calix slammed into the ground Avengers-style while Ascher hit Lex's soft back and slid off grumbling about gur in his mouth. I descended as well, just in time to see an Air Sprite's spear whiz by Calix, missing as he jumped back at the last second.

It seems that a note about Air Sprites would be appropriate here. Air Sprites are vicious creatures that look like what modern media has come to call ghosts. While they may look all wispy and mysterious, they are actually savage and their attacks very much do hurt. However, they are ghosts in the sense that most Air Sprites are the souls of people who have died airborne. Anyway, this Air Sprite was practically wrapped in air, with wind swirling around its body to make it 2 meters tall. It seemed more like a beast than a human.

It cocked its arm back, and another spear made of air appeared in its hands. It flew from the Sprite's hand towards me before it split into three, flying in separate directions and aiming for all of us at once. I quickly used my dagger to split the spear, the wind fragments flying back to the sprite. I looked over just in time to see

Ascher use his hunting knife to split the wind the same way I did. I didn't bother checking in Calix's direction because I knew he would already have dealt with the spear, one way or another. The wind cycled back, this time in the form of arrows. I shouted over the wind "Let's get this going!"

Ascher yelled out "Let's go!" As the arrows flew at us, we all rushed in towards the sprite, Calix closing in the fastest with his sword with me not far behind, dual wielding my dagger and shotgun. Ascher remained a step away with Mocha and Lex at his side, ready to cover the two of us.

I double checked that my job was still at Author before I yelled to Calix "My Shadows can't deal any damage to sprites because they are also considered as a type of Sprite! I'm fighting as a Reader now!"

Calix shouted back "Got it!" Before starting a familiar attack sequence. I was to support him with my shotgun and cover his back using my dagger while Ascher provided offensive support. Ascher darted in closer to us, sending Lex to help Calix fight. After a few beautiful arcs of his sword, Calix got in sync with Lex, alternating attacks from teeth and claws and a sword. Then somehow, I just knew that the Sprite was going to launch spears in all directions. I didn't understand how I knew, until I remembered that the voice of Areli had turned into my own thoughts. I screamed out loud "Flat on the ground!" Before assuming the position myself. I could see everyone, Ascher, Calix, and even Lex drop instantly to the ground. Then there were a series of whooshing sounds as spears of air whirled through the air where we were standing just moments ago. I could hear the crashing sounds from where the spears hit various objects behind us. More rubble fell from the buildings and the wind was soon hurling them at us again.

We all sprang to our feet again, dodging pieces of concrete and digging in on the offense. Then, I saw it. A window of opportunity. The Sprite's side was wide open as Calix was keeping it busy from the front while Lex attacked it from above. I saw an opening just as Lex swished past, jumping down on the Sprite from a large ledge to swipe with its paws. I fired a shot, expecting to draw some agro. What I did not expect, however, was for the Sprite to kneel forward, dead from a single shot of my bullet. I frowned. All I did was imbue the bullet with a little bit of my mana, not even a spell or a curse or an item. Ascher and Calix both stared at the now dead Sprite, looking at it with eyes filled with disbelief.

"Did you just one-shot a Sprite?" Calix asked, completely dumbfounded. I knelt next to the corpse and flipped it over. The Sprite's eyes were glazed and staring at nothing. I checked for its pulse. Nothing. It wasn't normal for me to be able to one-shot a Sprite, because we were only at the beginning few Quests. Logically speaking, it doesn't make sense. However, I couldn't show all of that because to them, I was a Reader, someone who had read the flow of time. So all I said in response to Calix was "Yes," My heart thudded in my chest, and I was worried he would ask how I did it. Thankfully, he just nodded and knelt beside me to examine the corpse. Ascher started chattering behind me about how cool and amazing it was that I could kill Sprites with one blow.

My lips were itching to tell some excuse about being lucky or hitting a weak spot, but I knew I shouldn't do that. Thankfully, Calix and Ascher both just seemed to acknowledge that I was strong and that seemed to be a solid reason for being able to kill Sprites like that. It was at that moment that I realized that they both trusted me. Like, really trusted me. My eyes welled up with tears as I thought about my argument with Calix a few days prior. However, before my tears even fell, we all got the notification for the next Quest to begin. I dried my eyes and schooled my face into a mask of cold. "Let's go," Calix said, and we all stood, just as the ground exploded with fire.

The next four Quest were all Elemental Odessies, following the same few phases and with the exact same Hacks. Each time, Calix and Ascher entrusted me to take care of the Sprite. Each time, we finished faster and faster, so by the time we were finished with the final Odyssey, water, we were able to finish in 6 hours.

We all sat down on the damp grass at the banks of Han River, soaking wet. I activated *{Blessing of Fire-Lv. 3}* we had all gotten from the 6th Quest and used it to dry Ascher before making sure all of my clothes and hair were dry again. "Well," Ascher said, smiling "That's over with. I wonder what the next Quest will be." His eyes bore into mine, as if begging for the answer.

I laughed, rubbing his head playfully. "I don't know if I wanna tell you that..." I joked, starting to panic a bit on the inside. Ascher started whining instantly. I called Calix through our connection. 'If I keep revealing too much information, there might be consequences from the Elves or Legends. Change the topic or do something so I don't have to answer him!' I let some of my desperation slip through. If I drew the suspicions of Legends or Elves, they may get Management involved. And once that happens, it's over. Calix seemed to understand what I meant as he stood up, stretched, and motioned for us to get up as well.

"What for?" asked Asher as he stood up. I saw him glance at me a few times and that was enough for me to know that he was feeling apologetic about the whining. I smiled at him, hoping to let him know it was okay. We'd both lost our childhood too fast, and I wanted to give him back the years of laughter and childishness he'd missed. I blinked hard, shaking away any unnecessary thoughts about the past. 'Move forward, move on.' I chanted in my head.

It seemed that Calix had tugged Ascher up onto the back of a Light Stallion in the distance. I laughed as I saw Ascher wobbling and almost falling off the Stallion as Calix started to run. I wanted to join them on Paragon, my Shadow Kelpie, but I didn't want to risk another collision of auras like before. I sent a warning message to Calix through our link. I saw, no, *felt* him give me a thumbs up. How was that even possible? I couldn't help but laugh at the strange feeling of receiving an invisible thumbs up from Calix. I sighed, shaking my head and carefully started to summon Paragon as well. I reined in my mana, making sure not to let any dark energy spill out further than an inch from either me or Paragon. Surprisingly, it seemed to work. No pain, no sudden wind. Calix and Ascher were still running by Han river, happy as could be. I swept onto Paragon's back and looked at the pair of them. The wind was tugging on Calix's silvery hair, begging for it to be set free from his tight man bun. Wisps of it were streaking out behind him, and Ascher was swatting silver hair out of his mouth, yelling something at Calix that I couldn't hear but made him smile and run faster. It all seemed perfect until you took your focus off of them and onto the landscape. I could see fires burning from the people still finishing Quest 6, could hear waves crashing against concrete as people fought off Water Sprites from the eighth Quest, could hear the roar of monsters as they fought each other.

The world was ending. But my world was still here. Still perfect. Still smiling like he should be.

Ch. 6

Era of the Dark Lords

A soft pop echoed through the air, now familiar to us all. I immediately looked over the new Quest window.

Quest-#9: 11 *Dark Lords-Lord of Hoard*
Difficulty: C+
Details: *Eleven lucky individuals will be chosen to become a lord? These lords will be granted immense power. Their job is to use their power however they see fit. Everyone else just needs to survive.*
Time Limit: -
Reward: -
Punishment: *Serve the Lord of the Hoard forever*

11 Dark Lords. The novel had called for 10 Lords, I was sure of it. So why the extra Lord? And why did the number 11 seem so familiar

to me? I ignored that feeling and turned to Calix and Ascher. "The Hacks for the next 11 Quests are simple," I said. "All we need to do is to find the Lords and kill them in the next 24 hours."

"Easy enough," Ascher said confidently.

"Not really though," Calix interjected "The Lord will likely receive the majority of their Legend's power, which will make them stronger than the monsters we've fought so far."

I noticed Ascher's face fall. His eyes began to fill with worry, glancing around as if the Lord of the Hoard could be anywhere. "But, that doesn't make them immortal or anything," I interjected, trying to put a positive spin on things. "We can still kill them just like anything else."

Calix smiled and drew his sword and the soft shink of it sliding out of its sheath sounded like a declaration of war against the Lords.

"Is there no way to weaken them, Astoria?" Ascher asked. "Like if we kill one, it'll weaken the others?"

I laughed aloud at that thought. "No silly," I said, roughing up his hair. "It's the apocalypse. They aren't going to make it easy for you."

"Right," Ascher said, stiffening up "The apocalypse. Right. No. That was a dumb idea."

Shit. I fucked up again. "No, I didn't mean that. I just laughed because it was a creative thought." I said to him, rubbing his shoulders. I shouldn't have laughed but it was such an innocent childish thought. To think that killing one might weaken the others.

Wait... Others. Why did that word seem so important to me all of the sudden? That's when it hit me. There are other people who've ready my novel. We called ourselves "The Others" and had long discussion in the comment section about the story. The name "Others" came from the fact that we all wished we were from other worlds.

Then, if there are 11 readers who completed AAE including myself, the author, and 11 Dark Lords... Then that could mean that all of the readers will become Dark Lords and have to be killed. Then that means... I might have to die for Calix to finish the Hack and help reset the world for Ascher. Or this could all be a coincidence and I could be over thinking things.

"Move forward, move on, move forward, move on. You can think of that later." I muttered.

Calix raised an eyebrow at me, but didn't comment. He just said "I'll start spreading a layer of my mana around to find the Lord." It was only a few minutes later that I realized that he trusted me to tell him what I was thinking about. He trusted me enough not to push or pry about it. Now, to most people, it might seem like common sense, just ignoring a muttered string of worries. But Calix? This is the same guy who, in AAE, skins a man alive for not telling him what he was muttering about.

I chose not to comment and instead focused on helping find the Lord as well. With Calix searching for any strong sources of mana and Ascher using his animals to locate potential Lords, I decided to use *{Memory of the World-Lv. 27}* to check the novel for information on the Lord of the Hoard.

{The Lord of Hoard is always someone who was poor, someone who was desperate to find more money, more food, more love, anything at all. That desire burned so bright that they were chosen as Lord of the Hoard, to be able to hoard everything they couldn't in their life before the apocalypse.}

Honestly, I didn't even need to use a skill to remember this line. I cried so hard the first time I reread what I wrote. I used to think that if AAE ever came to life, I would be the Lord of the Hoard. Money, food, love... Move forward, move on. I chanted in my head. There's no point reminiscing about the past.

"I got it!" Calix exclaimed, his voice uncharacteristically excited. "About 15 minutes from here on horseback, 30 if we go by foot. There's a young boy, maybe 13, who's mana is insanely high, like up in the high 5,000s." I quietly checked my own mana levels. 4865/4865. With Calix and Ascher by my side, it'll be an easy Quest to get over with. I got up onto Paragon immediately.

"I'll tell you the Hacks as we run," I shouted as I took off.

I heard Calix's distinct voice mutter "DAMMIT" just before I took off. I laughed as I watched Ascher and Calix scramble after me. Once we got into a steady pace running together, I started explaining the next few Hacks to them. Originally, the AAE had required Calix to have all 10 of the Dark Lords as his servants, all working for him and for the greater good of the world. However, it didn't have to be like that this round. While I was developing the story, I was always concerned about how the Dark Lords could have been killed and then Calix would have failed his Hack for that regression. I couldn't think of a way to balance the power between Calix and the Lords. There were moments when Calix wondered if he could ask someone to use a mind control or necromancy skill on the Lords so that he could ensure 100% loyalty. Eventually, one of the Lords did end up dying in a battle but was brought back to life using a necromancy skill purchased from the Astral Shop and that worked, and he would have completed all of the Quests of that world if he had been able to discover the Hack for one of the final Quests. Anyway, Calix ended up killing all of the Lords and bringing them back using more of the purchased necromancy skills. But this time, I was here, so I could just bring them all back alive and then give them to Calix.

To Calix and Ascher, I just said, "We need to kill the Lords, all of them, and put them under our control by using my necromancy skill. Then I'll just trap their souls in a bottle or something and give it to you, Calix. You have to be carrying the bottles for the Hacks to fully take effect, so make sure of that."

"So I'll be walking around with what, a dozen souls in my pocket? Amazing." Calix joked. "You know, it was my childhood dream to collect souls."

Ascher and I burst out laughing. Calix gave a sheepish grin. Calix was becoming more and more unlike the Calix I knew from AAE. That was something I'd have to admit. But I love the new Calix. He's caring, trusting, kind, and he jokes around with us and treats Ascher like his own sibling. The old Calix would have been cautious, serious, and he definitely wouldn't have trusted me OR Ascher. Character development, I thought as Ascher and I wiped our tears.

Soon, we arrived at the spot Calix had mentioned, and that's when we saw it. It was a mountain of food and cash and gold surrounded by an ocean of people. The debris from the destroyed buildings had been moved so that there would be more room for food and money. I pulled Paragon back into my shadow and Calix also dispelled the Light Stallion. I walked closer to the people and realized that they were all not blinking. It was like they were being mind controlled.

Ascher popped up beside me and whispered "They all look like zombies. Like they don't have thoughts."

Calix took up my other side. "They're probably being mind controlled," he whispered.

"What kind of mind control skill had this big of a range?" I asked, motioning around at what seemed to be thousands of people gathered in one place.

"Look," Ascher whispered, pointing at a man. He was middle aged with a slight pot belly, and not blinking. He just had this blank look in his eyes. He had his arms full of convenience store food and cash.

"There too." Calix whispered, pointing at a fit young woman in yoga pants who was dragging a cart full of what seemed to be enough jewelry for an entire shop.

"They're all bringing food and money and jewels to add to that pile over there." I whispered.

"It's probably a mind control skill of some kind, with the buff from the Quest making it so that it works over a wide range." Calix whispered. Just then, one of the controlled people stumbled into me. Or they would have if Calix hadn't pulled me closer to him at that moment. I stumbled right into his arms, surprised, as he continued the conversation like nothing had happened.

"It probably has a condition to be activated," he explained "We might have to be in a certain range to him or one of these other people have to touch us, something like that." He kept his arm around me, even though there wasn't really any one near us now. Even though he acted like it wasn't a big deal, I could see his ears reddening.

If this was the old Calix... No. I can't judge him by how Calix acted in the book. I have to just judge him based on the Calix I have in front of me. He likely just saved his Companion from a potentially dangerous situation.

"Is it just me," Ascher muttered. "Or has this area become really empty all of the sudden?"

I looked around and found that nearly all of the people

surrounding us were gone. There was a straight path from us to the huge mountain of stuff.

"Yeah, this definitely isn't normal." Calix said "Get ready, the Lord might approach us or attack." Somehow, he had positioned himself directly in front of me, placing himself between me and the mountain. I slipped out from behind him and took my spot next to him.

"You don't need to protect me." I told him, drawing my dagger. "We're Companions, remember? We'll protect each other."

"It'd be nice to have someone cover my ass too." Ascher joked as he placed his hand on a hunting knife while the other pooled with his deep green mana.

I contemplated, for a split second, whether I should fight as Author or Necromancer, but ultimately decided to stay as Necromancer, so that I could help push back some of the people in case they become a problem. A small part of me did want to switch to Author and start by physically killing the people in the way, but that wouldn't hold so well with Ascher here, so Necromancer it is. It was always easier for me to kill than to injure.

"Ready?" Calic asked.

"Born ready," Ascher replied excitedly.

Both me and Calix turned to look at him. "What?" Ascher whined "I've always wanted to say that!"

I was about to crack a joke about him wanting to be a super hero when I felt a shift in the air. A ripple of mana so strong it knocked multiple people off of their feet. I reached for my own pool of mana to throw up a shield before realizing that Calix had already done it. 'Over protective much?' I thought to him.

He threw me a rakish smile, then said out loud "Let's get closer to the mountain. The Lord is probably there." Together, we ran full pace towards the mountain and climbed to the peak of it. At the center, there was a large chair lined with velvet and painted gold. On it sat a thin young boy who was stuffing himself with food and his pockets with money. He didn't seem to notice that we were there. Quietly, I sent my Shadows to circle the base of the mountain, stopping anyone else from approaching and giving the Lord help. Calix drew his sword. Ascher tightened his grip on his hunting knife. That's when he finally noticed us.

He looked at us, saw we were empty handed and said in the calmest of voices "Get me more food and money. Then crawl somewhere and die." I felt a wave of mana wash over me, but I was otherwise fine. Then I saw Calix and Ascher both turn away, heading off of the mountain. I sheathed my dagger and grabbed both of their shoulders.

"What are you doing? We need to kill him now. He isn't that big of a danger, so let's get it over with before he gets stronger!" I exclaimed. Then I saw the look in their eyes. That same, empty look that the other people had. They were being mind controlled. But why not me? I glanced back at the Lord who had returned to stuffing himself, completely unbothered. That's when it hit me. I had the skill *{Mental Barrier-Lv. 7}*, which was stopping the Lord's skill from taking effect on me. I thought to Calix through our Companion bond. 'Wake up. Calix. Calix. Wake the fuck up." I could hear his thoughts clearly. He had let go of the barrier between us. Part of him was begging to listen to me while the other was chanting over and over to listen to the Lord's voice. "Wake up. You need to kill that thing so that we can get a move on with these Quests so that you can finally become the new Holy Knight, so that you can finally get your happy en-" Woah... Emotional overload. Okay. Chill. It's fine. You got this. I ignored Calix for now and turned to Ascher, still keeping a tight grip on both of them. "Ascher." I said gently. "Hey. Wake up. Wake up. Don't listen to him. He's the Lord, remember? We need to kill him. Ascher? Remember what we came here for?" I shook him gently but he didn't move, only stood, blinking with those glazed over eyes of his. That's when I felt someone staring at me and the prickling sensation told me that there was murderous intent behind the look.

I turned, still keeping hold of Calix and Ascher and found the Lord staring at me. He looked at me, then at Ascher, then Calix. "New plan," he said calmly. "Kill the girl, then get me more stuff." He was quiet for a second. "Oh, and then you can just stab yourself in some corner and die. But do it away from me so you don't dirty my stuff."

Calix's sword shimmered with his mana but something was wrong. His mana was flickering, like he couldn't decide if he should activate the skill or not. Ascher also stepped into a fighting stance with his knife. Lex and Mocha circled his feet, uncomfortable with fighting me. Okay, that was it. I quickly encompassed Calix into a bubble of my mana and put Ascher, Mocha, and Lex into another. I whirled towards the Lord and he was sitting there, just watching me. Then, staring straight into my eyes, he said in that same, infuriatingly calm tone of voice. "Everyone, give me what you are holding, then come here and kill this woman."

I could feel the gazes of hundreds, maybe thousands of people on me. I instantly went to work, sending Satan to organize the Shadows and make sure that no one could approach. I used more of my mana to levitate the bubbles into the air so that Calix and Ascher were out of the way. I could see in my peripheral vision that Calix was stabbing and slashing at my mana to no avail. Ascher was hacking at the bubble with Mocha and Lex helping him. I ignored them and approached the Lord. Mentally, I sent an order to Satan. "Aim to subdue but don't hesitate to kill." I barely heard his "Yes, my liege" before launching myself at the Lord. We tumbled off the chair and part way down the mountain before I stopped us. I held my dagger to his throat, pressing slightly so that there was a trickle of blood.

Even in the novel, the Lord of the Hoard was never a big issue to take down once you got him separated from the mind controlled people.

"If I kill you right now," I said "Will Ascher and Calix no longer feel the need to listen to you?" He didn't reply. His expression had turned from neutral into something more human. He looked vaguely afraid.

"I don't know," he whispered, his voice thick with emotion. He was shaking in fear now, shaking so hard he slashed himself across the neck one more time. "I don't know, I don't know, I don't know!" he screamed. He was going insane either from fear or from the power of being the Lord. I watched him struggle beneath me for a bit. "You know," I said quietly, "I do pity you." The boy stopped shaking from beneath me. His eyes were glued to mine, as if he would die if he looked away. "I pity that you had to live a life where you never had enough food, enough money. I pity you. From one desperate, starving person to the next, pity does no fucking good." I smiled down at him. "You'll be happier like this." Then I slammed the dagger into his throat and he died there, on the spot. I pulled my dagger out of him. I vaguely sensed that the people had all stopped fighting, so I called back my Shadows and released Ascher and Calix from their bubbles. Then I put my hand over the corpse of the boy. "To arms," I whispered.

Suddenly, the world went black. I didn't know where I was, if I was floating or standing or lying down. Then I started to see scenes flash in front of me, as if I were watching a movie, but there was no sound.

I was looking into a dirty mirror in a dark bathroom when I realized with a start that I was seeing things from the boy's perspective. I watched as the boy put on a school uniform for Evergreen Public Middle School. Then he pinned a little silver nameplate to the breast pocket of the uniform. The nameplate read Jay Park. That's when it hit me. This kid was web user "JayI$Rich". He was one of the readers who read AAE even after my 6 months of silence. I remembered talking with him in the comment sections of certain episodes, chatting about which characters were the strongest or best. Every time we talked, I thought that he had an odd obsession with how much Astral Coins each character had and now I realized that that was what had turned him into the Lord of the Hoard. I kept watching him as he walked to school, quietly attended classes, ate the free school lunch, stuffing himself full then asking for more to take home. I watched him return to the dingy old basement building where he set all of the food he had brought home on the table. Then I saw a man who looked to be Jay's father approach. He seemed to yell at Jay until Jay motioned to the food on the table. Then he instantly quieted and sat down to eat. I watched as Jay crept into a dark room and opened his phone to read the last episode of AAE. My heart thudded with fear as I saw him scroll to the end. He sat there and I could just tell he was happy and sad at the same time. Then, I saw the clock on his phone hit 10 pm. Saw him get the Quest notification. Saw him pick up an old baseball bat from the corner and beat the man to death. I could feel his happiness. He was absolutely ecstatic that he was in a world he knew, that he was in control. He went around stealing food, surviving Quests by just quietly hiding in a corner, all the while laughing as he watched others scramble around. He started to ask people for money and food in exchange for information on how to complete the Quests in the best possible way. Then he became Lord.

"Then I killed him." I muttered. It could be a complete coincidence that JayI$Rich became the Lord of the Hoard. Nothing to be worried about. I blinked hard and when I opened my eyes again, I was back on that mountain of food. But now, I had Jay's soul with me. I could feel the weight of a human soul in my shadow. I stood and waited as Ascher and Calix ran over. They battered me with a million questions from "Did you kill him?" to "How did you break the spell?" to "Are you okay?" That last one came from Calix and I was pleasantly surprised that he seemed to genuinely care. I quickly explained everything that happened from the mind controlling to the soul collecting. I did leave out the part about watching Jay's life though. That was for me to sort out. Almost as soon as I finished my explanation, a notification appeared in the air with the next Quest.

Quest-#10: 11 Dark Lords-Lord of Strife

Difficulty: C+

Details: One lucky individual will be chosen to become a

lord. These lords will be granted immense power. Their job is to use their power however they see fit. Everyone else just needs to survive.

Time Limit: - Reward: -

Punishment: Serve the Lord of the Strife forever

The people below seemed surprised to see that the Quest had been cleared. There were a few shouts from people as they realized that they could just hide safely and other people would clear the Quests for them. This was true for the next few Quests, not that it would matter soon. "We have the same Hack this time," I said "So let's just relax for a bit." I sat down on the mountain and picked up a random apple, polishing it with my shirt before biting into it with a satisfying crunch. Calix immediately flopped down next to me and started to look for something to eat as well.

Ascher, who was understandably confused, asked "Don't we have to look for the Lord this time?"

I motioned for him to sit down next to me as I explained "The Lord of Strife feeds on strife and can create strife. People will start becoming irritable and they'll start to fight each other over the pettiest of reasons. Wherever there is the most fighting, the Lord of Strife will be there. Just his presence will be enough for most people to start fighting each other."

Calix frowned. "What if we start to fight each other? It's not like you can maintain a bubble for that long and I can help as well."

"So can I," Ascher added immediately.

"Well..." I started. After explaining my plan to them, we all got ready to move. "Calix," I called.

"Yeah?"

"Here." I said as I placed a small, pure white stone into his palm.

"What is it?"

"It's Ja-, it's the Lord of Hoard's soul, condensed to the form of a stone."

"Thanks." He shoved the stone into his pocket. "Ready?"

"I was born ready." I said, mimicking Ascher's voice.

"Hey!" Ascher protested, "I do not sound like that."

I gave him a patronizing "Of course," which earned me a smack from Ascher.

"Let's get on with it," Calix groaned but I caught a glimpse of a smile on his face before he turned away.

I got into position across from Calix. He bent his knees and drew his sword, grinning like a mad man. "Oh stop that will you?" I chided as I tilted my head, listening for the distinct sound of Lex, Ascher's wolf, howling which we had agreed upon as our signal. Calix gave a little laugh but did as I asked.

I drew my own dagger, blowing some mana into it. I feel a change in the air tell me that Calix had also blown some mana into his sword. That's when I heard it. A long howl that echoed through the empty buildings. Stray dogs peeked their heads out and started howling as well, aroused by the howling.

I couldn't help the grin blossoming on my face as Calix launched himself towards me. His sword was shimmering with his mana and he let loose a scream as his sword hit my dagger straight on.

"Come on," I taunted, "I'll make sure to control my strength for you."

A competitive fire lit up in his eyes. "Let's see how long till you're begging at my feet." He snarked as he lunged for me again. I side stepped, then went on the offense, wielding my dagger just using the {Sword Dance Lv. 20} skill. We went blow for blow for several minutes, trading loud insults but playing I Spy with our Companion Bond.

I almost fumbled it once, saying "I spy with my little eye..." until I realized I had said it out loud and finished with "...an imbecile who needs to learn his swordsmanship again!" I couldn't meet Calix's eye because I knew that if I did, I would burst out into laughter and our plan would be done for.

Soon, I heard little yips echo over the pavement. I couldn't tell if it was Mocha or Lex, but either way, yipping meant that the Lord was near, that he was almost in our bait. That's when I activated *{Memory of the World-Lv. 28}* Calix must have felt the change in my vibe because he shut down the bond.

I launched myself at Calix, using my copied *{White Star Sword Aura-Lv. 10}* to attack him viciously from everywhere. Calix stumbled a bit but managed to fend off my attacks pretty well, probably because he knew the skill. I pressed harder, using more and more of my mana now that I knew he could take it. I was about to unleash my next series of attacks when I felt a sudden sense of peace and calm wash over me. I didn't even realize I had let go of my dagger until a few moments later. So this was Ascher's skill.

He told me that the skill was called "Mediator" and it made people calmer and less likely to fight, but I didn't know it would feel like this. Any way, everything was all going according to plan. I encase Ashcer in a bubble again and zipped him to where me and Calix were. "Where it it?" I asked the moment he landed.

"Behind that building." Ascher replied, pointing. "He was just about to feed on you guys' strife when I used *{Mediator}*. I saw him collect strife from the air like it was mana or something,"

"Alright, we'll sneak up and kill on my count okay?" Calix ordered, taking charge. "Take 3 minutes, spread out but don't be seen. First person to get a visual sends a soft mana ripple."

"Aye, aye, Captain," I said, giving him a mock salute. Ascher copied me, taking up the army stance and salute.

Calix made a shooing motion, laughing, before he leapt into the air and disappeared out of sight. I sprinted towards the building, ducking into a corner behind a stack of rubble. I could see Ascher running in the opposite direction, taking up position towards the right. I could feel Calix's mana on the floor above us, rippling out in soft waves. I scaled the wall of the building, trying to get into a good position to get a visual.

When I pulled myself over the edge of the next floor and found myself face to face with a woman my age.

{This world was never fair, but the apocalypse made that even more clear. If the Lord of Hoard got what they wanted the most, the Lord of Strife is forced to be the person they hate the most. To put it plainly, the Lord of Strife is someone who hated any type of fighting. Once they become the Lord of Strife, they feel physical pain whenever they see strife. Yet the pain gets better each time they feed on it, creating immunity to the pain they feel. They eventually begin to seek out strife on their own, completely disregarding their morals from before the apocalypse.}

The woman I saw before me was huddled in a corner, crying. She looked so weak. It made me question how she had survived until now. But I could tell from the mana pulsing from her, the mana that was growing every moment, that she was the Lord for this Quest. She looked up and saw me. I could see Calix from behind her, approaching slowly. She was still crying when she stood up and started swinging a knife wildly at me.

No. Her knife was calm, cutting through the air with a precision that could only be manifested by someone who has had years of practice with one. I fended off her attacks with my dagger, trying to defend myself while moving away from the edge of the building. As we fought, I could tell that her eyes were crazed. She was sobbing and screaming in a way that made it obvious that she was in immense pain even though I had only been able to scratch the surface of her skin.

I could hear sneakers slapping concrete and I knew Ascher was taking the stairs up. The woman, the Lord, turned to the sound. Calix took that as a sign to draw his sword and leap at her. Lex rushed in from somewhere and started helping, biting and clawing at her ankles. I also ran over and helped, stabbing her in a few choice places. That's when I noticed that she wasn't fighting back. She was curled up on the floor in the fetal position, covering her vital spots with her arms and legs. Calix seemed to notice at the same time I did. By then, Ascher had made it up the stairs.

"What's going on?" he asked "Why is she like this?"

"I don't know." Calix said, poking her arm with the tip of his sword. "She was fighting us just a moment ago, then she suddenly curled up like this."

"Then can't we just kill her now?" Ascher asked, drawing his hunting knife.

"Yeah," I said, "I think we can. Just be on the ready though, she might suddenly fight back."

Calix imbued his sword with more mana and I pulled out my shot gun, just in case. Ascher walked over so that he was behind her and placed the tip of his knife on the back of her throat. "On three," he said. "One, two-"

"Three," whispered the woman. She spun around so fast that I didn't have time to fire a shot or take a stab at her. She grabbed Ascher's knife hand and used her own knife to stab him in the stomach. My vision went red as I heard Ascher's pain filled scream. I was firing at her before I knew it. Two clean shots into each of her thighs. I made sure that she couldn't wrench the knife out before catching both of them and dragging her away from Ascher. I hesitated for a moment, unsure if I should check on Ascher or get my revenge on this bitch first. Then I noticed Calix who was running over to us. I made the choice then.

"Calix, get your ass over here and take care of Ascher." I yelled. My blood was boiling. I could barely recognize my own hate-filled voice. I stuck my gun back into the holster and used my free hand to slam the bitch against the wall. I threw her down to the floor and sat on her stomach. She was sobbing again and the sound was driving me fucking mad. "Shut the fuck up!" I yelled at her. She kept sobbing but it was quieter now. I grabbed her right hand by the wrist. "You thought," I began, "You could just sit there and gather more strife, didn't you?" I used my dagger and sliced off her pinky. She screamed so hard and thrashed like a fucking fish out of water. My ears started ringing. Finally, I screamed "Be quiet" and slapped her across the face, the sound ringing out over the now-quiet building. I realized that Ascher could probably hear me, so I used some of my mana to cover his ears only, preventing sound. Calix would be fine hearing this. In fact, he needed to. He needed to understand just how important Ascher was to me. He was the one that had said he wanted to be honest with me and trust me after all.

I returned my attention to the sobbing wrench beneath me. "You thought you were so smart, didn't you?" The right ring finger. Another round of screams and sobs. "Everyone here," Middle finger. "Knows that you" Index finger. "Can't feed and fight at the same time." Thumb. I grabbed all of the dismembered fingers and shoved them in her mouth. She started to choke on her own flesh and blood. "If you promise to stay quiet," I whispered "I'll take the fingers out." She started nodding her head off. Annoying as fuck, but whatever. I opened her jaw with more force than necessary. I heard a small crack that probably meant I dislocated it. I used the tip of my dagger to fish out the fingers one by one. Then I turned to the left hand.

"Where was I?" I contemplated, tapping my chin with the flat side of my dagger. "Oh yes. I was talking about how you thought you could out smart us but had to resort to pulling dirty tricks to fight, acting all defeated and broken then doing a surprise attack." Left pinky went flying across the room. A scream that was cut off with a sharp look from me. "Now that you've hurt my brother," Ring finger. "I'll return the pain tenfold." Middle finger. Index finger. Thumb. She let out a scream so shrill and loud that even Ascher, in his comatose state, flinched. My anger rose to even taller heights and I slapped her again before reaching into her disgusting mouth and grabbing her tongue. Seraphis seemed to know exactly what I wanted and slithered down my arm and set it on fire. I was almost thrown off of her stomach as she bucked but I held fast. After about a minute I removed her charred tongue from her mouth with one quick flick of my dagger hand. Then I climbed off of her and slammed my dagger into her stomach, the way she did to Ascher. I repeated that same stabbing motion again and again and again. I tuned out her screams. All I was aware of was the number of times I had stabbed her and the white-hot fury boiling in my stomach. I knew she was dead by the fifth stab but I didn't care. I kept going until I'd stabbed her ten times. "I always pay it back tenfold." I whispered, wiping her blood from my face.

I removed the cover I had over Ascher's ears and made my way there. Ascher's face was pale, and he was shaking a bit. I saw that Calix had used several potions and a couple tins of something to help. He had also ripped his own shirt to stanch the bleeding. It was now haphazardly discarded in the corner and Ashcr's wound was cleanly dressed with cotton bandages, the knife still in there, stuck up to the hilt. "How is he?" I asked Calix, my voice calm again.

Calix didn't mention my fit of screaming rage or my destruction of her corpse. Instead he just muttered "He's in critical condition.

I poured as much healing potion as I could down his throat and slapped 2 tins of salve over the edges of the wound itself before I bandaged it." Then he muttered something so quiet I couldn't hear him

"What?" I was annoyed he was muttering to himself about something that could be concerning Ascher.

"You could have left some for me," he said, louder. It took me a moment to process what he had said. I laughed a bit, then immediately felt bad for laughing while Ascher was potentially dying in front of me because I couldn't protect him.

"My apologies but I can't help but think that I've let you take the much more important task of tending to Ascher." I snipped back.

"Geez, relax." Calix said "I was just joking. I got to see you take enough revenge for the both of us. Which was pretty fucking hot by the way."

"What?" I asked, dumbfounded. "Did you really just call me hot over my injured brother's body?" Calix's face reddened and he started mumbling again. Ignoring him and the strange pounding in my chest, I bought a few items from the Astral Shop. For once I ignored the notifications buzzing in my face. I opened the bottle of {Healing Potion of the Elves} and poured as much of it as I could down Ascher's throat. I could hear Calix muttering something about a potion worth a thousand coins, which had been earned over the course of 4 Quests. I barely registered what he was saying though. A thousand thoughts were swarming in my head.

Did I really just let Ascher get stabbed in front of me? I should have fought as Necromancer and had my Shadows guard him. No, I shouldn't even have let him take the kill in the first place. He should have been the furthest away from the Lord when we attacked. I should have thought of a better plan, one that placed him further away from the fighting. In fact, he shouldn't even have been part of the plan. No, he was smart and he had powers, so he could have helped. But that help should have stopped at using his {Mediator} skill and then taking cover. No, there could have been better, safer ways for him to be a part of the plan. He's a fricken Carnivore Communer, even though he is good with that knife, that should have been a last resort. Necromancers, Mages, Communers, Summoners, and Healers are all roles that should be at the very back of the attack team, every team game I've ever played, every web novel I've ever read told me that. Hell, even a middle schooler would have had more common sense than me at that moment. God, I'm so dumb.

"Hey, hey! Astoria!" Calix shouted, shaking my shoulder. "You okay there?" I immediately reached for the Companion bond between us and slammed it shut, blocking communication from both sides. God, the bond was open while I was spiralling, so he would have heard me lose my shit. Well, he's also seen me lose my shit and absolutely mangle that body, so who cares at this point. Also, I'd come to trust Calix to have my back. That's why I asked him to take care of Ascher while I got my revenge. If it were any one else, I don't think I could have trusted- No. I know I wouldn't have trusted them to take care of Ascher.

I decided to be honest with him and said "I was just spiralling a bit. Thanks for pulling me out."

"No problem" An awkward pat on the shoulder. He stood and gave me a hand. "Let's find somewhere for Ascher to rest. I think he should get more potions and salves and maybe new bandages every few hours. We don't know what was on that knife of hers."

"Yeah, okay" I used *{Blessing of Earth-Lv. 3}*, which we had all earned during the 7th Quest, to create a platform under Ascher. Then I used *{Blessing of Air-Lv. 3}* from the 5th Quest to carefully pick up and move the platform.

"Where to?" Calix asked, using his mana to bring the corpse of the dead Lord with him. I thought for a moment.

"Let's go to the nearest hospital we can find. It'll have at least a few good beds and hopefully some clean sheets and bandages in case we run out of Coins."

"Okay"

We walked like that in silence, just me leading with Ascher next to me and Calix following. He didn't ask where the nearest hospital was or what our next steps were going to be. He just followed me, blindly trusting me. We finally found a small hospital that wasn't completely destroyed. We entered the part of the building that was still standing and found ourselves in the children's ward. There were several small, decaying bodies that had been crushed under rubble or had died due to their IV drips being disconnected.

"Fuck," Calix whispered. The word echoed on the broken linoleum floors and cracked titanium walls. "The doctors and nurses, those bitches..." The tiny bodies were still here but no adults in sight. They'd left the sick children to save their own lives. It was the first time I'd seen Calix swear so openly. He really loved children. The novel- No. I knew he loved children because of the Calix I see right now, the one who was getting angry for the sake of children he didn't know. Without thinking, I reached over and grasped his hand, unfolding it from the tight fist he had been making.

He froze for a moment under my touch, but slowly, he unfurled his hand and laced his fingers through mine. His hands were large and rough, filled with callouses and cracked from lack of proper moisturization. That's when it really hit me that Calix was basically half naked. He had ripped up most of his shirt to stanch the bleeding earlier. I could see his pale, defined abs and half a pectoral. Honestly, I may or may not have spent a moment or two just then, appreciating the view.

We kept walking through the halls like that, Ascher first, on his bed of flat stone, then us, then the mangled corpse. Together, we looked like a zombie parade, with me covered in blood and Calix's shirt ripped. We found an empty room on the second floor that was left relatively untouched, not too much debris, no blood or bodies either, Carefully, I moved Ascher from the slab of stone I had him on to the hospital bed. A wave of my hand, and the stone slab was dust. Calix dumped the corpse in a corner as far away from the bed as possible. I set up some basic barriers with my mana, using the elemental skills I had, then adding a layer using pure mana.

I broke the silence first. "We still need to get through the Quests, but we can't leave him like this." My mind was honestly blank. I was desperately hoping for Calix to give me a solution as I avoided his gaze with just as much desperation. Calix moved next to me and, without looking at me, placed an arm over my shoulder, pulling me closer to him. His arm was muscular and hard, but it made me feel safe and comfortable in a way I hadn't felt in a long time.

"I'll hunt the rest of the Lords. You only need their bodies, right? I'll bring them here and you can turn them into Soul Stones while you care for Ascher." He said softly.

I turned and stared at him in shock. "You would do that? But would you be okay? I mean..." I couldn't finish the sentence, but the rest of it was clear as day. I was the one that had caught the two Lords so far, with Calix and Ascher providing little to no aid each time.

"I know that I haven't been much help these last few Quests." Calix said firmly, turning to face me as well. "But I need the fighting, the experience, so that I can protect the people that matter to me. And so that the world doesn't end. So trust me. I can do it."

I nodded slowly. Solo hunting the Lords would definitely be a challenge for Calix at his current level, but it would really help him increase his skill level and stats. "Be careful, okay?" I asked. I hesitated for a second and put my hand on his cheek. It was warm against my cold, pale fingers. "Life and death in the apocalypse can be decided by even the direction of wind. You don't know which breath will be your last." I pinned my gaze to his deep blue eyes, crystal clear and bright. "Promise me you'll come back."

"Of course Astoria," he whispered, stepping closer to me until his face was only a few centimeters from mine. His blue eyes seemed to pierce me. His gaze softened as his eyes met mine. Then gently, he placed a feathery kiss on my cheek, soft and careful, the way you would kiss a baby. He turned and left without another look or a word, but I swear I saw his ears and cheeks redden as he left.

The door clicked softly behind him and I carefully brushed my own fingers against my cheek where Calix's lips had rested just a moment ago. My hand felt ice cold compared to his hot touch. I can still smell the residue of him in the air. Crisp sage with notes of warm cedar wood. I can feel the heat on my cheeks and I know I'm blushing. This was stupid. I'd known him for less than a month. A coy little voice purred in my head. "You've read and dreamed about him for 8 years of your life though." That was also true. A line of AAE suddenly popped into my head.

{Calix Nerezar is destined to never find love. Calix Nerezar will always believe in and hope for true love and love at first sight.}

I couldn't help the smile blooming on my face as I turned to Ascher again. My smile fell almost instantly as I gave him a closer examination. His forehead was burning up with a fever, so I covered him up with more blankets. Carefully, I began transferring my mana to him to help the healing process. Since he wouldn't swallow more mana potion, this would be the fastest way to get him back on his feet.

But of course I couldn't just force my own, purple mana into his body, which could only use green mana. So I began the painstaking process of matching my mana to his, one shade at a time. The tone and shade of your mana is decided by your identity, by who you are. But you could mimic someone else's mana by thinking of them, of their personality, characteristics, and even their odd little quirks. Since I didn't know how big his mana pool was and I didn't want to waste my mana, I decided to make an IV drip of mana so that more could funnel in as he used it to heal. I found an empty one in a room not too far away and brought it over to Ascher's bedside.

His breathing was still unstable and he was sweating hard. The wound itself shouldn't be causing these effects, so I had to assume that the blade was poisoned. That bitch. I glanced back at the mangled corpse, wondering if I ended it too quickly.

Yeah. I definitely did. I opened the top of the plastic bag and poured my mana into it. It manifested in the form of a purple liquid with swirls of black in it. Exhaling a breath, I focused my thoughts on Ascher as I dipped a finger in the mana. The liquid was cold to my touch and seemed to prick me. It stung a bit but that didn't matter.

I closed my eyes gently. Let's start with his appearance, I decided. Soft, curly hair the same shade as mine, with eyes that were a warm brown color. His nose was long and rounded and his upper lip had a scar on it. His skin was slightly tan with a few visible muscles from his hours playing soccer with his friends. He was tall but not too tall, probably only a few centimeters taller than me. He was kind and soft hearted, but if he needed to, he could be firm and speak his mind. He was the most precious person in the world to me. I opened my eyes again.

The mana in the plastic pouch had turned a deep green. It was almost the exact same shade of green as Ascher's mana, maybe one or two shades lighter. It would be close enough. I closed the plastic bag and hung it on a hook on the wall. I inserted a little tube at the bottom then screwed on a small needle at the end. I was no nurse or doctor, but since this was mana, it wouldn't really matter where I poked the needle. I decided to do it on the back of his hand, slowly sliding the needle into one of the surface veins. As I opened up the flow of the IV drip, the green mana trickled into his hand, the vein was glowing softly, emitting a greenish light. I watched his face carefully, worried that the mana wouldn't take. Thankfully, he didn't seem to be in any discomfort. In fact, his face seemed to relax as I increased the flow, the mana taking the edge off of the pain and helping him fight the poison. I watched him for a few moments before I peeled myself away from him.

I reopened the Quest window for the 11th Quest. I think it arrived sometime while I was torturing the body of the Lord. The window reopened in my vision. It read:

> *Quest-#11: 11 Dark Lords-Lord of Seduction*
>
> *Difficulty: C+*
>
> *Details: One lucky individual will be chosen to become a lord. These lords will be granted immense power. Their job is to use their power however they see fit. Everyone else just needs to survive.*
>
> *Time Limit: - Reward: -*
>
> *Punishment: Serve the Lord of the Seduction forever*

I almost laughed out loud. I had sent Calix to kill the Lord of Seduction...right after our first kiss. Technically, it wasn't even a real kiss though, just a peck on the cheek, but it seemed more intimate than any other kiss I'd had before. I've had a couple boyfriends but no one had ever been able to make me feel so much by doing so little. I blamed the apocalypse for heightening my emotions. But the Lord of Seduction... According to AAE, the Lord of Seduction looks different to everyone, shapeshifting to become their exact type from eyes to hair and even their voice. Then they would release a pheromone that would make people want to- You know what? I think this is enough. I shook my head a little and turned my attention to the corpse in the room. Okay, focus. I stretched my hand over it. "To arms", I said quietly.

Again I was transported to that movie theater type place. This time, I was in the perspective of the woman. Her day started out normal. She lived alone in a little apartment, had an office job at some tech company, and a decent lifestyle. Nothing too out of the ordinary. Except for every little bit of tension at her job, any one fighting, even the street cats, she had to stop and settle it peacefully. I could feel that she really felt good doing that. I could physically feel happier, lighter when I saw her do that. She was innocent, smiling, the type of person other people couldn't easily get mad at. She reminded me way too much of Ascher. Dammit. No. This bitch was nothing like Ascher. I kept watching as she flopped onto her dull bed and opened her phone to a familiar screen. AAE. I glimpsed her ID as she logged in.VanessaKim. Just that clean first and last name. No other special characters or even numbers. Just her name. She was the one that never commented, only liked every single episode. She only commented a handful of times to break up an argument in the comment section between other users. She was nice. Always calm, always the mediator who stopped fights in the nicest way possible, even if it meant people swearing at her over the internet.

She was the kind of person who didn't seem real. Yet she always acted in the same, predictable way. It was almost like she was an NPC in a game, programmed to stop every fight she saw.

I opened my eyes again. This time, I barely felt the weight of the soul in my shadow. I quickly condensed the soul into a stone. This time, it was a stone, a shade of light gray, almost like a cloud. I fingered the stone. Vanessa. She was so nice. No. Nice doesn't quite capture it. She reminded me of a young lamb. Pure, innocent, and having never witnessed what might happen beyond the safe fencing of a farm.

I stood up and added more mana to the pouch, forcing it to mimic Ascher's dark green color before allowing it to touch the existing mana. It got much easier after the first time. I paced the room, having nothing to do. Every once in a while, I topped up the pouch or adjusted his blankets, not daring to touch him in case it hurt. I hated feeling his sense of helplessness, but I couldn't just leave Ascher here and go hunt Lords like nothing had happened. Plus, I trusted Calix to be able to handle the situation. If he needed help, he could always call me through the companion bond. Then I received a new Quest, this time for the Lord of Hell. My heart was thumping loudly on my chest. Calix had managed to clear the Quest solo.

These last few Quests have gone without much intervention from the Legends. Considering how the Monarch of Souls even came into my dreams during Quest #4, His power must be dwindling. That or the Greatest Fragment of Divinity is keeping a close eye on him. Both of them aren't a good situation. It's been a whirlwind of a week since the Selection, and I realized that this is the first time I've been able to really calm down and analyze the situation.

A slight pop startled me out of my thoughts and I realized that the Quest window had automatically disappeared. Almost immediately after, I heard Calix through the bond. "Took care of the Lord of Seduction. I'll drop by the hospital with the body before I go after the Lord of Hell." I flicked my gaze over to the new Quest window, still open at the corner of my vision.

Quest-#12: 11 Dark Lords-Lord of Hell
Difficulty: C+
Details: One lucky individual will be chosen to become a lord. These lords will be granted immense power. Their job is to use their power however they see fit. Everyone else just needs to survive.
Time Limit: - Reward: -
Punishment: Serve the Lord of the Hell forever

"Okay," I told him. "You're okay, right? No injuries or anything?"

In the few seconds between my careful question and his answer, my heart practically jumps up and lodges itself in my throat.

"I'm fine." Calix said and I can almost see the crinkle at the corner of his eyes as he laughs. "I have a few scratches from those steel nails of hers, but I'm alright."

"Good," I said, trying not to let my voice waver.

"How's Ascher?"

"Getting better. I put some mana in an IV drip for him, and don't worry-I already purified it to the point where it's only one or two shades lighter than his."

"Of course." A beat or two of silence. "How are you faring?"

"Me?" I asked, startled. "I'm fine. I'm not the one that got stabbed. I'm also not soloing any Quests right now. I'm fine." I expected him to smile, maybe a laugh, but I didn't feel anything through the bond other than worry.

"Not physically."

I knew what he meant. He saw me flip out and then break down in the span of a few hours. To be honest, I was trying my best to ignore it, to focus on something else, but the guilt was gnawing away at me. "I'll get there." I said quietly, even though I wasn't sure if I'd ever stop blaming myself for the scar that'll most definitely be on Ascher for the rest of his life.

I felt Calix trying to comfort me and I smiled a little. "Come back quickly, alright?"

"See you in a bit."

I fidgetted around for a few minutes. Add more mana to the IV, increase the flow, wipe off some sweat, re-bandage his wounds and put more salve. Had Seraphis burn off the blood stains in the corner of the room. I did consider buying an antidote for the poison, but using the wrong antidote could make the situation worse, so I just let it be. I plopped down in the middle of the room and decided to organize my thoughts a little.

The Monarch of Souls was losing power, and the Greatest Fragment of Divinity gained it. I knew that it was because I was only the Monarch's pupil while Calix was the successor of the Holy Knight. If I gain more power, it'll hopefully help balance things out between the Legends. But that's a big if, so my current best shot at tipping the scales is to remove Calix. I brushed my hand over my cheek again. No. No. That's not happening. Besides, if I did take Calix out of the picture, that would mean that most of the Holy Knight's power would be lost while the Monarch of Souls' power would grow. That is the scenario that the Monarch of Souls wants and the Holy Knight would want it vice versa. But me? I would never truly be happy in a world where either the Shadow or Light Force reigns.

Even while I read AAE, I'd always had a little voice at the back of my head that wondered why there even had to be different Forces, why everyone had to pick a side. I knew it was a naive thought, to think everyone could live in peace. But it seemed so ridiculous that these almighty beings were so set in their ways that they couldn't see that peace was possible. I knew the story of course. I read it in AAE, where the Greatest Fragment of Divinity told it to Calix Herself.

The Legends all choose a successor in each version of the universe in a never ending attempt to return to the Nether. All Legends, at their core, are ghosts of people who existed, even in some far off universe that no longer exists. They became too famous, their legend told too many times, for them to be forgotten by humanity. So they stayed here, instead of moving on, trapped in the Ether, Realm of the Real. However, if they can find a suitable successor through a series of trials, a new soul could take on the role. The leader of the two Forces were always Legends who hated each other for one reason or another. This led to the two Forces not wanting to see each other in the Nether, so they grew their power in the hopes of being able to trap the other Force in the Ether for good. The Nether is a place where all the fallen Legends are, a place where they are able to observe the happenings of the Ether and "live" in a paradise. The longer a Legend remains in the Ether, the more desperate they are to escape it. At the end of the chapter where the Holy Knight explained all of this to Calix, Someone had left a comment "Damn... Good to know that the Legends are just a bunch of suicidal ghosts... Fuck I love this story." 10 likes.

I fingered the cloud gray stone in my pocket. Even with me observing these people's daily lives, it's hard to know the details. If they had family or a lover, if they were awaiting a big promotion, if they had good friends... Also, the fact that the Quest window keeps saying 11 Lords. The two so far were both readers of AAE; they'd been reading it when this mess began, so they'd obviously read it to the end. 11 Lords. 11 readers of AAE. I'm probably going to be one then.

I stared out of the shattered window, a slight shimmer beyond it, the only evidence of the complex shields that lay beyond it. I looked through it at the burning city. The sun was just beginning its descent from the sky, lighting the city with an orange glow. There was still chaos everywhere. People desperately fighting for their lives against the Quests, the monsters, and the insane odds. The monsters were still out there, hunting and killing. But what if... What if there was a monster on this side of the barrier too?

I won't let Ascher of Calix see me broken. I won't hunt them. I'll just try my best to die without hurting anyone then Calix can... Shit. I can't live with my soul bound to Calix. Wait but if we're already Companions, doesn't that mean... Because I have a duty to protect him...No. I can't risk all of our efforts with the Hacks going to waste because of me. I have to have a sure-fire way, just in case I'm one of the Lords. I can't ask any Shadow Force Legends to help me because they'll likely bring me close to the Sharpest Embrace of the Night.

The title I had chosen for Death.

I also can't ask any of the Light Force Legends, because they'll be suspicious as to why a necromancer, obviously of the Shadow Force, would want to sacrifice themselves for the Holy Knight Successor. If anyone asked me why, I would tell them it was for Ascher, so that Calix would keep protecting him even when I'm gone. But the honest truth is that I don't want to see this Calix turn into the Calix I saw in AAE. The one who had lost his humor, the one who had lost hope. He nearly went insane in one of his worlds and I don't want that to happen to him. He doesn't know how much pain he has to go through just to become the Holy Knight. I hope that I'm the last Lord to be turned. That way I only have to find one way to turn a dead soul into a soul stone without a necromancer. Or... I could find a necromancer. I shook my head, there's no way I could find a necromancer. Besides, I have to stay with Ascher, make sure he's safe and he can make it out.

I got to my feet and left the room, making sure to add more mana to Ascher's IV and another layer to the barriers. I walked around the empty hospital for a while, looking for something. I found it at the reception desk on the first floor. A notebook and a pen. It wasn't anything special, just a black ballpoint pen and a leather, lined notebook that could fit in your pocket. I tore the used pages out and stuck the pen and notebook in my pocket. I went back up to the second floor and sat at the edge of Ascher's bed and started writing.

It was nearly dark when I felt it. A familiar presence at the door. I jumped to my feet, pocketing the pen and notebook. I whirled to face the door. It clicked open slowly and Calix was there, leaning against the door frame. He had a few long scratches on his limbs and torso, his face was flushed, and his shirt was slightly torn, revealing a set of sweaty abs through the slit. I managed to keep my eyes from lingering too long, although Seraphis did start squirming on my arm.

"You're back," I said, relieved to see he was safe.

"I am." He replied simply.

"You have the body?"

"I do."

"Same corner please." The body whooshed through the air at the speed of a bullet to the corner of the room. I didn't even bother to look at it and just grabbed a tin of leftover salve for Calix's scratches. "Take your shirt off."

"That eager, huh?" He said slyly.

I threw a surgical towel at him from a nurse's cart. "Take it off and wipe that sweat off while you're at it."

"What if I said that the scratches hurt when I try?"

I sighed and handed him the tin. "Hold it." Honestly, I was eager to get a better look.

I made my way to him and, without touching him, put a layer of my mana over his skin, beneath the wet, torn shirt. Seraphis, who had been wriggling all over my arms with excitement, finally calmed down enough to set Calix's shirt on fire. The fabric burned easily off of him, the ashes clinging to him. I removed my mana from him and with it, the ashes. Then I had that same mana used to activate {Blessing of Air-Lv. 3} to dry his sweat. I glanced at him and saw a genuinely annoyed look, which nearly made me burst out laughing. Then he caught my eyes and I did. He looked startled at first but joined in.

"I expected this to be a good opportunity to feel your touch, but you never cease to surprise me, Astoria." He said, wiping tears from his eyes.

"That's me," I said as I motioned for him to hand me the salve, "Full of surprises." He was quiet for a moment as we stood there. Him without his shirt and me putting salve on his scratches. I was screwing the lid of the salve tin back on when I noticed a spot in the room with unnaturally dense mana. It was familiar, cold, icy white. Calix's mana. I glanced over there and it was the corner where he had dumped the body. It was covered in a thick stone wall from floor to ceiling. "What's this?" I asked, mildly amused.

"Uhh..."

That's when it hit me. The body of the Lord would be in the same form as when they died, the form of Calix's ideal type. Yeah, okay, I see why he has the wall up. To be honest, I was really curious to see what his type was, but I also didn't really want to know. We'd gotten a lot closer this past day, from the adrenaline or maybe from the thought that this is our only chance to find love in the apocalypse. I didn't want to let that break. This new relationship between us was progressing at a dizzying pace, not to mention one of us is a character from a book who believes in love at first sight while the other is a human. It's the apocalypse though. Who gives a fuck if we date after a week of knowing each other?

Woah, where did that thought come from? I just turned, as nonchalant as possible, to face Calix, who was blushing profusely. "I...Uhh...So, it might come as a bit of a shock beca-"

"It's fine," I said lightly, cutting him off. "I won't judge your tastes." I walked to the wall and gave Calix what I hoped was a reassuring smile. He did hesitate for a moment, but ended up removing the wall. Lying there, crumpled on the floor, was the body, crumpled and bloody. I straightened the body so that it was leaning against the wall facing me. I avoided looking at her face and decided to focus on the other parts of her first. She was dressed... minimally, so to speak. No. Let's be honest, all she had on was a scrap of black fabric that barely covered what needed to be. I blushed faintly. There was a deep, bloody gash on her chest, presumably what killed her. Her hands had claw-like nails that were made of steel and the size of my forearm. And her face... I stared at it in shock. Then back at Calix, who was turning a shade of crimson. It was the face I saw in the mirror everyday. It was me.

The logical part of my brain worked desperately to find a plausible excuse. He could have cast a veil over it to throw me off. There's no logical way that he's actually in love with someone he met a week ago, right? Fuck. That. Shit. I wasn't thinking any more. It was him for me this whole time. For 8 fucking years. I loved him, feared him, cheered for him, supported him, cried with him, and thought about him all the time. And that was when I didn't know he was real. Who cares if this is dumb and we were at each other's throats a few days ago? I love him and he clearly loves me.

I jumped up and threw myself at him. He caught me and the comforting scent of sage and cedar wood surrounded me. He rested his head on mine and that's when I realized just how tall he was. I pulled back just a little and told him straight up. "I love you." It wasn't a question. It was a statement. A fact. The truth.

"Love you more." The truth.

—--

It's been a little more than a week since Calix and I started officially dating. During that time, Calix kept soloing all of the Lord Quests. We were now at Quest #18, Lord of Chaos. Things were going smoothly. Ascher was up and moving again, begging to go out of the hospital that had become our little haven. I was also starting to go a bit insane, staying inside except to go find food when we didn't have coins and to fight some random monster that was getting too close. We did end up revealing to Ascher that we were a "thing" because having secrets in a group when you're a part of the same group could be fatal. He teased us endlessly for the past 4 days, really ever since he's been up and running.

Honestly, I'm so glad he took it okay. I was worried he wouldn't like the development between us. Between me and Calix, there wasn't really much difference, other than soft little kisses at night and meaningful touches here and there. Calix was sweet and over protective and getting stronger with every Quest. Which brings me back to my biggest issue-I still haven't found a solution as to what to do once I become a Lord. Calix is preparing to hunt the 10th Lord, the second to last. That means I'm the 11th. Every single soul I'd collected so far had turned out to be one of the final readers of AAE, so it's certain that I'm next. My best shot as of now is to make sure Ascher stays inside the hospital while Calix kills me. Then I'll just have to make a bet.

I fingered the notebook in my pocket, the leather one I'd found after the end of the 11th Quest. Over the past few days, I'd filled it out with all of the Hacks for the rest of the Quests as detailed as I could. What needed to be done. What the easiest way to do it is. What the potential consequences are. Et cetera. I wanted to make sure Calix could save this world and become the next Holy Knight.

The Monarch of Souls would be furious if he knew, yet I had a small feeling that he already did and he was waiting to see how far I took it. "Oh, game on," I whispered.

"What was that?" Calix asked, looking up from cleaning his sword. He was leaning against the far wall, next to the window going through his usual routine of cleaning his sword.

"Nothing, nothing," I said, waving him off. Ascher and Calix shared a look and started shaking their heads in unison. I smacked Ascher on the shoulder lightly like I was annoyed, but in reality, I was enjoying this. These rare moments of joy. Me lounging on the bed with Ascher and Calix going through his own routine like always. It seemed like a sliver of peace compared to the world outside.

"Astoria?" Ascher began in the whiny tone he used when he wanted something. "Can I please please please-"

"Get to the point Ascher," I said, already expecting his answer.

"Can I go and help Calix with the 18th Quest?" he said quickly.

"Like I said," I began, slightly annoyed. "It's only been about five days since you were up and moving again. Plus, this is a good opportunity for Calix to get stronger-by facing Lords on his own. After this, the Quests will get harder and it-"

"Then shouldn't he get stronger now since he's going to face harder Quests later?" Calix interjected.

I turned to face him, letting him see the annoyance on my face. "You're siding with him too?"

A shrug from Calix. "I mean, it can't hurt to get stronger, can it?"

"And he can do that while training with me, safely, while you finish up with the Lords on your own."

"Astoria." This is from Ascher, and his uncharacteristically serious tone of voice makes me pause. "You can't protect me all the time." He begins "I know you want to, but that's just not possible any more. And that's okay. Because I can get stronger on my own now. Getting stronger through the Quests will help so much more than just training."

I study Ascher's face for a moment. This is a new side of him that I've been seeing since the apocalypse started. This firm side of him that tells me directly what he wants and why he wants it. The side of him that makes me realize that he's not the lost 13 year old he was a few years ago.

"Okay." I said finally "You can go, but only if-" I stop myself as Calix and Ascher cheer. Going to high five each other like they've won a sports match or something. I smile at them. My two favorite people in the world. I would do anything to give them a happy ending to their story, to their world. Even if that means I won't be there to see it.

Soon after, the two left to finish the 18th Quest and I was left alone. I decided to leave the hospital as well, gathering all of my belongings. I left the notebook and pen on the bed, where it would be noticeable. I didn't write any explanation or clue as to what would happen in the 19th Quest. At the threshold of the room, I turned back and looked at the room that had been our home for the past week or so. A hole on the wall from when Ascher put a fist through it when he heard Calix and I were dating. A singe mark on the wall near the door from when I almost burned Calix because he'd entered the room without warning while I'd been asleep. I told myself that these weren't tears welling up in my eyes. As if by denying their existence, I could somehow lessen the sorrow I was feeling. Steeling myself, I made my way down the linoleum halls and down to the main entrance of the hospital. The moment I stepped beyond the barriers, and dispelled my own mana armor, the monsters whirled towards me. I doublechecked that I was in Author before throwing myself at the monsters. I needed as many monsters slayed as possible if I was to increase my odds of successfully dying later. 'The hot liquid running on my face isn't tears. It's sweat.' I told myself. I was soaked in equal parts sweat and monster blood when I finally stopped.

I wandered from the hospital then, moving further and further away from it, killing any of the monsters I saw along the way. Then I found myself a small mountain of rubble to stand on, make myself more visible for when the 19th Quest started. I entertained myself by messing around with my skills, doing useless things like making tiny cities of dirt then running mini floods, fires, or tornados through them. Stupid and pointless, but it killed time.

30 minutes. I stripped myself of weapons, throwing my dagger and shot gun away from me with all my strength. One hour. I cut the companion bond. I didn't just slam the door between us shut. I burned the door. The sweat on my face is because I expended too much mana.

I was just approaching the half hour mark when the notification arrived. There was no warning. Just the notification in front of me.

Quest-#19: 11 Dark Lords-Lord of Willful Ignorance

Difficulty: C+

Details: You have been chosen to become a lord. You will be granted immense power. Use your power however you see fit.

Time Limit: -

Reward: -

Punishment: -

As soon as I finished reading the Quest window, I could feel a wave of power shock me. It was painful. Insanely. I couldn't help screaming. I barely registered that my abilities had all doubled and my mana, which was near empty just a moment before, was now fully charged.

After nearly a minute, the pain receded. I had this odd sensation like I wasn't in control of my own body. It felt similar to what I felt when I turned the Lords' souls into soul stones. I started walking and I caught a glimpse of my reflection on a window. I looked like me, except that my hair was longer and my eyes were completely white. I could tell that I was walking towards a hiding place for a group of people. Only one or two people in each country ever actually managed to make it past Quest #30, mostly because everyone was too busy hiding and trying not to get eaten to worry about the Quests. A wave of my hand blew the door off of a small building. I could see that there were two families huddled inside, shivering in fear. Another flick of my hand and they all collapsed on the spot. Their eyes were also glowing and most were crying. That's when I realized what I'd become. I was the Lord of Willful Ignorance, a Lord with a mental attack skill that made people admit what they'd been willfully ignoring. I didn't feel anything other than hunger looking at the family. 4 adults. 3 children. Shivering in fear. All I felt was hunger. I breathed in deep and I could feel myself getting stronger, could feel the desperation of those people take the edge off of my hunger. In the span of two minutes, all 7 people had died, their minds breaking under the pain. I left the house, but not before I saw myself in the bathroom mirror. I was covered in black blood from the monsters I'd killed earlier and my hair was streaming behind me even though there was no wind. My eyes were glowing white and I... I looked like a monster. No. I couldn't let Ascher or Calix get hurt by me. I walked outside and saw shards of glass littered on the ground below my feet. I willed myself, I desperately ordered my body to bend and pick one up but I just kept walking. I kept trying every time I saw something sharp or dangerous but always to no avail. I could sense that I was heading towards the largest source of mana around. Calix. The ice white aura and scent of sage and cedar wood. I used to find those sweet and comforting, maybe even hot. Now, all I felt was hunger. As I walked, I kept feeding on the nearby people. Call me inhuman but I didn't waste my efforts trying to save those people. I already had two people I was failing to protect, I couldn't add more.

That's when I saw them. Calix and Ascher. They were walking towards me, Ascher tracking me with mana, not realizing that I was the Lord. I could see the confusion on their faces when they saw me. Calix's sword was dripping with blood and he still had the body of the Lord of Chaos, so I knew that they didn't stop at the hospital. Good. They didn't see the notebook yet. Didn't see that I knew it would happen. I could feel my arm raising, my mana getting ready to break their minds. Calix was still talking to me and Ascher was still making his way towards me. It was like watching a movie without sound. I knew Calix was talking but I couldn't hear him. I could see Ascher shouting but I couldn't hear him.

I desperately willed myself to stop. To lower my arm. To stop my mana. To stop hurting them. I saw it on Calix's face just as I was a second away from using my skill. I saw it in the way his eyes were running with tears, the way he bit his lower lip and set his jaw. Crying, he launched himself at me, sword high. Ascher was screaming, crying, yelling over and over the same word I was screaming at myself. To stop. I was using a set of skills I never had before to fight Calix sword to sword. A black sword had manifested out of nowhere and I was fighting him with a sword skill I didn't have.

Calix was crying, still yelling. I could make out my name on his lips. I kept fighting with my body, trying to stop myself from fighting him. Calix hadn't even activated any skills. He wasn't attacking but he also wasn't giving me any room to use my feeding skill again. Ascher was trying to push us apart with his animals. Then he used his {Mediator} skill. It bounced from me. Ascher used it again and again as we fought. I knew they could do it. Kill me.

Finally, Calix activated his *{White Star Sword Aura}*. I wanted to smile at him. To tell him it was okay. To tell him that he'd find someone else. Ascher had a nosebleed from using his skill too much. I could feel it. Could feel my strength leaving me, could feel my mana draining. Calix never once stopped calling me. Ascher too. Even as he fought me with his skill, I knew that he didn't have any killing intent behind it. They kept screaming. Kept calling my name. Kept crying.

I'll admit it now. I wanted to cry. I wanted to sob but I couldn't. I also wanted to smile because they would make it. They'll find my notebook, where I told Calix to ask the Holy Knight to turn the Lord of Chaos into a soul stone. For me, I was willing to take a bet.

I had gotten stronger with the buff from the Quest, but Calix and Ascher were desperate. They were fighting with all of their strength, slamming down mana potions as the minutes passed. We were nearing two hours of our 2-on-1 fight when I felt it. I was out of mana and insanely fatigued. So when Calix made a stab at my chest, the same stab I'd dodged or deflected for the past two hours, I didn't have enough mana to maintain my sword. My sword dissipated and I fell forward, all the strength leaving my body. I fell straight onto Calix's sword.

I could hear again and after two hours of silence, Calix's scream was painful to hear. It was a sound filled with pain and fear and horror. I smiled weakly. My vision was blurring and my stomach felt like it was on fire. I could hear Ascher yelling. "Astoria! Astoria!"

Then Calix's urgent "Healing potion Ascher, now!"

"It's useless," I whispered. "Look at me, I'm a kebab on your sword." I coughed and couldn't stop the blood spurting from my lips. Calix was cradling me.

He kept whispering. "It's fine, it's fine. You're gonna be okay. I love you so much. Everything's gonna be okay."

"Calix." I said, my voice fading. "Calix. It's not your fault. Whatever you think, it's not your fault. And... and I love you... so much."

Calix shushed me. "Stop talking, don't waste energy. You're not dying. I refuse to let you die."

"Calix. Shut up." I said, my voice barely audible even to my own ears. "This is the apocalypse...people are always...dying. This isn't... different. So... protect who you can. Ascher, where's Ascher?" My vision was completely gone now, Calix's face was a blob of white and blue. Whether it was pain or tears or incoming death I didn't know.

"I'm here, I'm here." said a blob on my left.

"Ascher, Ascher. Shh... You don't-" A cough so painful I'm pretty sure I fainted for a moment or two. I could feel the blood running from my lips. I wanted to wipe it away, but I was struggling to stay awake let alone raise my arm. "You don't have to cry. You don't have to blame yourself or Calix. This... was for... the best...okay?"

"No, no, no!" Ascher screamed "I'm not losing you. I'm not- I'm not going to watch you die!"

"I love...you both...okay?" I whispered. My arm slipped from Calix's hold and hit the ground. I could hear screams. Then blackness.

Ch. 7
Eye of Terror

Blip! Blip! Blip!

Strange. I died, yet I'm still getting notifications from the system. Wait. I'm dead. I died. Calix killed me for the 19th Quest. How am I thinking? And I was aching everywhere but that meant I had a body. Slowly, I pried my eyes open. A familiar tile ceiling. A creaky bed that smelled of bleach. I was at the hospital. I tried to sit up and my whole body protested. I grit my teeth and pushed myself up. Then failed to maintain my balance and plopped right back down with a soft "Oof."

"Astoria?" asked a familiar voice.

"Calix?" I muttered. Suddenly a face popped into my vision. It was Calix. His eyes were puffy and his clothes soaked with blood, but it was him. Then a second head popped up next to him. Ascher. His eyes were red and his face was tear streaked but he was here.

"Astoria!" Ascher screamed.

I winced at the noise. "Too loud," I whispered hoarsely.

"Sorry," Ascher said. "I'll go get you some water," he sprang up and ran out the door. Not 5 seconds passed before he came back with a cup full of water. Calix helped me up to a sitting position against the pillows before taking the cup from Ascher and helping me drink.

I sunk back against the pillows, exhausted.

Calix carefully peeled back the blankets and I was too tired to ask what he was doing. Then I heard the gasps. I looked down and saw that the hole in my abdomen was gone. Clean. My skin, flesh, and organs were all there, like I'd hadn't been stabbed. Yet there was a hole in my shirt the size of a sword.

"How are you-" Calix began.

"Gimme a minute," I replied, too exhausted to care for manners. I opened all three notifications and read them one by one.

Hidden Quest: Life For Lives

Issuer: Monarch of Souls

Completion Condition: Kill exactly 11,111 beings

Beings Killed: Chimera x2, Dragon x3 ...Human x7, Ant x1

Reward: One extra life, courtesy of the Issuer. (Soul will be restored to previous body)

Catch: Ownership of said soul will go to the nearest living being.

Reward for Hidden Quest: Life For Lives has been given.

Owner of Your Soul: Calix Nerezar.

Quest-#20: Eye of Terror

Difficulty: B

Details: Whatever you do, do not move.

Time Limit: Set to begin in 24 hours 14 minutes and 9 seconds. Completion time may vary.

Reward: -

Punishment: Explosion of your soul

What? The last kill on the list was an ant, and I only received this after I died. So that means that in the last few minutes of my life, I killed an ant. When did I... My arm. Calix lost his grip on my arm and I let it fall to the ground. My hand must have hit an ant. I could help but smile as I told Ascher and Calix the exact situation. Ascher kept hugging me and saying, "It worked out. You're okay. Everyone's okay." as if reassuring himself. Calix was strangely quiet.

"Hey Ascher," I said, disentangling myself from his arms. "Could you give us a minute?"

He glanced between the two of us. "Yeah, of course. I'll be in the building. Holler when you guys are good."

I gave him a quick smile and he left the room. "How could you do that?" Calix asked immediately, his voice hard.

"I'm sorry, but that was the only way I could save you two."

"By taking the risk on your own and not telling the rest of us?"

"I'll tell you everything now."

"Be honest. Did you know that this would work? That the Monarch of Souls would issue a Hidden Quest to save you?"

"I didn't, but the odds were worth betti-"

"Worth it? Nothing is worth your life, Astoria. Nothing!" He was nearly shouting now.

"You are." I said quietly. "Ascher is."

He just stared at me. "I'm going to let this go just once, because you came back to me. But I'm letting you know that the Holy Knight told me that the Monarch of Souls is likely taking you as his successor. I've known since after the Aether Odyssey. Yet I still loved you, still trusted you, knowing that you lied to me." A desolate little laugh. "This is why I love you. Because I know you'll love me. I'll let you keep your secrets. I won't ask any more. But you promise me that you won't pull this shit again."

"I promise." Calix pulled me into a hug and kissed me over and over. Sage and cedar wood and salty tears.

"I missed you so much. I was so scared you wouldn't- Oh Legends. I... I love you so much, Astoria. I really do." The truth.

"I love you too." The truth.

We spent the day resting and recovering. Ascher was happy to see us back to our "normal, sappy selves" as he put it. After some food and a couple mana potions, I was back in pristine condition.

We went to bed early that night, Ascher and Calix dragging over a second bed so that we could all sleep at the same time. So far, we'd been sleeping in shifts with me and Ascher sleeping during the day while Calix was out hunting Lords then Calix crashing alone at night while me and Ascher trained and hunted. It had been a long time since the three of us could relax. We talked for a while that night, just lying there together, looking out of the window at the night sky that burned. We pretended they were stars. Then we fell asleep.

I knew this was a dream from the weird sensation of it, the way my body seemed to lag behind my thoughts. I was alone in the dark. Then I wasn't. The Monarch of Souls appeared in front of me, and I couldn't speak. I was forced to kneel at his feet, silent. "You realize that at this point, the only way you can avoid getting yourself killed at my hands is to make it to the end of the Quests, right?" *He asked. I could feel the rage in his words. I couldn't move a muscle, couldn't nod or say yes. He seemed to know that and continued on.* "I'll try to help you, but you have such preposterous ideas that I'm not sure how much I can protect you. Use your resources well. Your phone is in your pocket next to the notebook, which they never saw." *Then the darkness swallowed Him, and it swallowed me too.*

When I opened my eyes, it was around noon. The end of the 19th Quest didn't shorten my hair again, so it was long to the point where it was brushing my tail bone. I had decided to keep it at this new length. I was braiding my hair when Ascher and Calix walked in, smelling of sweat. "Oh good, I was just about to wake you." Ascher said. "We have about 15 minutes before the start of Quest #20 and you didn't tell us about the Hack yet."

"Right, right." I said, standing, "Honestly, the Hack for this Quest is simple-you have to participate in the Quest." Calix had made his way behind me and was finishing my braid for me. "All you have to do is be eligible for the Quest."

"How do you not participate in a Quest?" Calix asked.

I took a deep breath. "The Quest transports people who love each other into a room where one by one, they are shown one of the people dying. It will feel real. All of your senses will tell you that it's real, that you can sprint out there and you can save them. But they aren't in any danger. They'll be right across from you, watching you watch a holographic video of them die. Some people can't participate in this Quest because they don't have anyone they love or anyone that loves them." I twisted a little to look at Calix's expression. He seemed unbothered by it.

"That won't matter then," Ascher says "Because I love you, not in a weird way, and Astoria loves you, so Calix is fine."

"Right." I said firmly. "So all you need to do is close off your senses and keep telling yourself that it isn't real."

"Don't worry," Calix whispered in my ear. "I know you love me, so I'm not afraid."

I gave him a light kiss. "Whatever you do, just don't move."

A few minutes later, I was pulled into a black hole and deposited in a dark area. There was nothing but darkness and a glowing circle beneath my feet, just big enough to stand on. Then two more circles appeared in the distance, one ice white and the other forest green. The one below my feet was electric purple. The circles seemed to move closer together until we were no more than two meters away from each other. As soon as the circles stilled, a glass triangular prism rose from below. The prism was a mirror, showing a reflection of me. Then it showed Ascher. "Whatever you do," I yelled. "Don't leave the circle!" Then the prism exploded. There was a blinding flash of light.

When I opened my eyes again, I was back outside, in a building. It was the same one where Ascher got stabbed by the Lord of Strife. My body seemed to move, but I wasn't moving, like when I became the Lord of Willful Ignorance. I made sure not to step out of the circle. I "walked" to the exact spot where Ascher got stabbed and I watched it happen all over again. Me telling Ascher he can finish the Lord. Him approaching her. Then the countdown. One, two, stab. But this time, I didn't leap to save Ascher. The Lord pulled her dagger out of him. He was bleeding out, dying there on the floor. Somehow, both the Lord and Calix were gone. Ascher was begging me to help him to please save him.

It felt real. I could smell the blood in the air, feel the slight wind on my face. I could hear Ascher, his painfilled voice begging me to help. I stood there, motionless, not batting an eye at his desperate screams. A minute passed, then two. The fake Ascher died. A full minute passed before I felt a sensation like being sucked back. Then I was back at the prism.

The prism was made of clear glass now, so I could see Calix and Ascher's relieved expression as they looked around, checking to make sure everyone was still here. Honestly, the vision shook me. I was refusing to help Ascher when he was injured. Not unable to, refusing to. The look of desperation and betrayal on his face was heart breaking. The prism changed again, showing my reflection. Then it warped and showed Calix. The prism exploded again and this time, when I opened my eyes, I was at the place where I died. I watched as Calix and I fought again. Ascher was nowhere to be found. I watched as Calix and I fought again. But this time? It was me who stabbed Calix. My sword went through his heart and out his back. Calix spurted blood, coughing. He kept asking me why I was doing this. And that's when I saw it. My eyes weren't white and my hair wasn't long and floating. I had stabbed him with a dagger and not a sword.

I was me. Just me. I wasn't a Lord yet and I had killed Calix. I used my foot to push Calix off of my sword and started stabbing him with it. All throughout Calix just kept saying "It's okay, I love you, let it all out." I almost stepped out of the circle then. I wanted to close my eyes and cover my ears with my hands but I didn't dare move, afraid that I would run out of the circle if I did. I could still smell the blood in the air. Feel it hot against my skin whenever it spurted from Calix. His eyes were glazed with pain when I finally stopped, smiling down at his mangled body. "I'm glad you're happy now. Love you so much" He whispered. Then he died. The scene stayed frozen like that for a minute. Me, smiling down at Calix, covered in blood and mangled. Calix smiling up at me, telling me he loves me through the pain. I could taste the blood in my mouth now, coppery and hot. Then I was sucked backwards and thrown back into the dark room.

The coppery taste still remained and I realized that I had bit my lip too hard. I knew in my mind that this was all a ploy, that the point of the Quest was to drive people insane after throwing them on an emotional rollercoaster. I knew. It didn't make the videos any easier to see. I checked that Calix and Ascher were both okay. They both seemed shaken and Ascher was pale but otherwise they seemed fine. My turn. The clear prism turned reflective then, showing my face. Then it split into two, one side showing Ascher and the other Calix. In both of them, they were watching my fight against Calix as the Lord. Calix had his eyes closed and was singing a song. I wasn't sure, but it sounded like Riptide by Vance Joy. I turned to Ascher's screen.

His eyes were locked on the fight. I opened my mouth to warn him not to move, but I couldn't make a sound. He watched himself, helpless to stop the fight between me and Calix. Then the video approached the part where Calix stabbed me. I could tell that Ascher had placed himself in the situation. He was leaning dangerously close to the edge of the dark green circle, which flickered and pulsed, as if anticipating his fall. Then just as my sword disappeared, Ascher took a step, stretching his hand out as if he could stop it. I tried to scream. I leaned as far out as I dared to and banged on the glass showing him. It was like I was watching it happen in slow motion. The front of his sneakers hit the rubble, then the back. He had half his body out of the circle when Calix stabbed me. I could hear him shout "No!" Then his entire body exploded. I shoved all my mana at the glass, my rage, my panic. I didn't have to though, because immediately after all three of us were thrown forward.

I found myself back at the hospital room. Calix was here, he was fine, but Ascher. There was a splat on the ground. Blood and gore where he stood. His head was there. On the floor. His mouth was still in an O shape, his eyes frozen open. "I can fix it. I can fix him." I said into the silence. "I can bring him back." Calix whispered, giving me a tight side hug.

"No, babe, you can't"

"Yes, I can. I'm a fucking Necromancer." I yelled pushing him off me. I stretched a hand over... him and yelled "To arms!" Nothing. Again. "To arms!" Nothing. "To arms."

"To arms."

"To arms."

"To arms."

I kept going until every last drop of my mana was gone. No. No. No. "It's fine, it's fine." I said aloud. "I died and came back, so there needs to be a way for him to..." A line from the Quest window seemed to flash before my eyes.

Punishment: Explosion of your soul.

I had written that line myself.

{Explosion of your soul is the truest form of death. There is no coming back from it, because everything that was you, your memories, habits, emotions, everything that made you you was gone.}

I lost him.

I lost him.

I lost him.

He was gone. Ascher. My Ascher, my only family, gone. 'Because you failed' whispered a voice in my head. 'You killed him. You made this world. You created that Quest. Wrote it with your own hand. You killed him. You monster."

No. No. This can't be happening. He was 16. 16. What world lets 16 year olds just... die? He didn't even love. Never had a job. Never drank. The world is full of things that he didn't do and now, he can't do any of them. This world is fucked up. What kind of world lets an innocent 16 year old die, right? I'll burn the world for letting him die. Then I'll burn too, for letting it happen. I promise, Ascher, I'll make them burn. The truth.

Epilogue-Calix

When Ascher... yeah. I felt lost. I wasn't a stranger to pain or grief. I had seen an entire world, my world, end after all. But this... his hit different. And Astoria.. She was just staring down at... it was like she had lost the world. I heard her mutter "I promise." Her voice sounded so small, so broken, so lost that I went over to hug her again. That's when she started screaming.

I'm not sure I have the words to explain what it sounded like. It was animal and filled with pain. It seemed to echo across the entire world. It sounded so broken, so desperate, so full of pain. I wanted to comfort her, to kiss her and tell her it's okay, we can grieve together. I could hear her fear, her despair, her anger at everyone and everything. I had my own grief, but it felt like a drop of water compared to the ocean of emotions she was screaming. Finally, she stopped screaming and slumped down against the wall.

Her eyes had this empty look to them, like she had screamed out all of her feelings. The look on her face made me feel like the world was ending all over again. I had just watched my world crumble and break under a mountain of grief. I wanted to help her. I wanted to protect her. But I had no clue how. She looked so small, so broken. I wracked my brain for something helpful I could do. That's when I noticed the bloody mess on the floor.

He deserves so much better than this. I burnt all of his... remains and put it in a glass jar made of my own mana. The most beautiful jar I could make for the purest soul I knew. Then I stuck it in my pocket. It's a good thing I did because next thing I knew Astoria had burned down the whole building.